Gra X-SS
Grape, Jan.
Found dead in Texas

$ 25.95

Found Dead in Texas

Found Dead in Texas

Jan Grape

Five Star • Waterville, Maine

Five Star First Edition Mystery Series.
First printing

Published in 2002 in conjunction with
Tekno Books and Ed Gorman.

Set in 11 pt. Plantin by Minnie B. Raven.

Printed in the United States on permanent paper.

Library of Congress Cataloging-in-Publication Data

Grape, Jan.
    Found dead in Texas / Jan Grape.
        p. cm.—(Five Star first edition mystery series)
    ISBN 0-7862-4841-6 (hc : alk. paper)
    1. Detective and mystery stories, American.   2. Women
private investigators—Texas—Austin—Fiction.   3. Austin
(Tex.)—Fiction.   4. Texas—Fiction.   I. Title.   II. Series.
PS3607.R425 F6 2002
813'.6—dc21   2002029944

For Karla, Phil & Roger
Extraordinary human beings
and delightful offspring
of whom I'm very proud
and for Mari.

Acknowledgments

The title of this book came about some 12–13 years ago when Mari Hall and Paul Youngblood and I were in Philly at a Bouchercon and discussing a name for a new Sisters-In-Crime Chapter. Paul says the name was his idea, I thought it was Mari's, but we know she adopted it and it became Mari's trademark. Mari lost her struggle with breast cancer in 2000, but when I was searching for a title, *Found Dead in Texas* popped into my mind. I contacted Paul. He was pleased and thought that Mari would be also. Thanks Mari, and thanks Paul. A big thank you to Marcia Muller, for her friendship and inspiration. Thanks to Mary Smith, editor and friend. Thanks to Ed Gorman for writing advice, friendship and for laughs. Thanks to Bob Randisi for writing help and friendship. Thanks to Dominick Abel for taking care of business. And last but not least, thanks to Elmer for always being there.

Table of Contents

Introduction

by Marcia Muller

When I first met Jan Grape at one of the many mystery conventions we attended in the late 1980s, she introduced herself as both a fan and an aspiring novelist. We soon became good friends, and I wasn't at all surprised when, in 1990, she announced yet another incarnation: co-owner, with her husband Elmer, of a new book shop in Austin, Texas, Mysteries and More. Over the years that followed, she channeled her boundless energy and enthusiasm into hand-selling books for grateful authors, publishing short stories, and pursuing her dream of becoming a novelist.

2001 was a milestone year for Jan. Her first novel, *Austin City Blue*, featuring exceptionally likable and clever policewoman Zoe Barrow, was published by Five Star. And now we have her first collection of short fiction, including nine of her best stories. As the title suggests, they are regional tales set in the state she knows so well and peopled with characters who reflect the manners and mores of their place and times.

Five of the stories showcase Austin private investigators C.J. (Cinnamon Jemima) Gunn and Jenny Gordon. The partnership and friendship between a black and a white woman mirrors the changing relationship between the races in contemporary Texas, and Jan explores the issue of discrimination on the basis of both race and gender in a thoughtful but never heavy-handed manner. In "Whatever Has to Be Done" and "A One-Day Job" the partners investigate murders that appear to be family affairs. A killing takes a personal turn for C.J. in "Kiss or Kill," Jan's first mystery story, published in *Detec-*

tive Story Magazine #4 in 1988. Simple disappearances are never what they seem in "Scarlett Fever" and the Anthony Boucher Award winning "A Front Row Seat." And in a most unusual tale, "Kittens Take Detection 101," Jenny's cats, Nick and Nora, help her crack a case in her own neighborhood. Interesting: the last time I saw Nick and Nora they were sleeping beside Jan's computer!

A very different kind of partnership is that of Robbie and Damon Dunlap, the heroes of a pair of stories in these pages. Damon, sheriff of fictional Adobe County, is often aided by his mystery writer wife in solving his more intricate cases. In fact, Robbie's insights into the human condition and tracking down of clues would put a less confident lawman to shame. Damon is proud of his wife's abilities, however, and in "Arsenic and Old Ideas," the first appearance of this detecting duo, he gives her the credit she is due. "Ruby Nell's Ordeal" gives further testimony to the old adage that behind every great man is a great woman.

Zoe Barrow, heroine of *Austin City Blue*, made her first appearance in "The Man in the Red-Flannel Suit." An officer on the Austin Police Department's RPO (Repeat Offenders Program) unit, Zoe has good reason to be lacking in the Christmas spirit: husband Byron is in a nursing home in a coma after being shot in the head in the line of duty. But the kindness and charity of the season prevail as she goes to the aid of a frightened little girl and finds her life taking on a new and better direction.

Enough said; it's time to let the stories speak for themselves. I know you'll enjoy Jan's explorations of the people and places of the Lone Star State as much as I did.

Marcia Muller
Petaluma, California
March 14, 2002

Whatever Has To Be Done

A fierce lightning and thunderstorm jarred me awake at 5:12 a.m. Autumn storms in Houston, Texas, often give the impression the end of the world is near. The dream I'd been immersed in had been pleasant, but try as I might, I couldn't remember it. The brilliant streaks flashed a sesquicentennial fireworks display and seeped through the top edge of the mini-blinds as Mother Nature declared a moratorium for sleepers.

It's not in my emotional make-up to wake up early; neither alert nor cheerful. Maybe it has to do with one of my past lives or blood pressure slow down or something. Anyway, I tossed around trying to will myself back to sleep, knowing all the time it wouldn't work. But I waited until seven to crawl out to the shower. "Damn Sam," I said aloud, while dressing and wishing I could have my caffeine intravenously. "Lousy way to start a Friday."

The pyrotechnics were over, but the rain continued steadily, steaming the interior of my car and making the rush hour drive to the LaGrange building hazardous and hair-raising. Determined to shake off frustration at the lack of sleep and the Gulf Coast monsoon, I paused in front of the fourth floor door and felt a sense of pride as I read the discrete sign—G. & G. Investigations. My partner, Cinnamon Jemima Gunn, and I could be proud we'd turned a profit the last three months. No one expected it to last. Sometimes, even we had doubts.

There was a message from C.J., as she was known to all except a few close friends, on the answering machine.

"Gone to Dallas for the weekend, Jenny. Work today and play tomorrow. Keep outta trouble, Girlfriend." She had a legitimate reason to go; a dying client wanted to find a missing niece and a good lead led to "Big D", but once the work was done, she had a friend playing football for the Cowboys who would show her a fun weekend.

Lucky sister, I thought, ready to feel sorry for myself. "But wait—there's only a half day's work here," I said aloud, "and it's rainy—and besides it's Friday." It only took two seconds to decide to finish the paperwork and to blow this joint. I put myself in high gear and was ready to leave by noon.

I had straightened up the lounge/storeroom, grabbed my purse and reset the phone machine, when the outer door opened.

"Oh. No. Don't tell me you're leaving?" the woman said. "Are you Jenny Gordon?"

She was slender with reddish blonde hair; not really pretty, her eyes were too close together and her mouth too thin, but there was something about her. Vulnerability? She had one of those voices that rise into a whine and grate like fingernails on glass. I hate voices like that. She dropped her dripping umbrella, one of those bubble see-through ones, onto the floor. Her raincoat, after she peeled it off to reveal a blue velour jogging suit, hit the sofa and slid to the floor. I hate slobs, too. As if your things are not good enough. Maybe people like that just don't care. Or maybe she was used to someone picking up after her.

"I am Jenny Gordon and I was leaving, but what may . . . ?"

"Well, great. That's the way my whole life has been the past twenty-four hours. All screwed up." She walked over and sat on one of the customer chairs, rummaged in her purse for a cigarette and pulled out a lighter in a silver and turquoise case. "It's really the shits, you know. Me needing a P.I." She burst out laughing in a high-pitched nervous tone.

I tried to figure out what was going on without much luck.

She stopped laughing long enough to say, "And who does he send me to? A woman, for Christ's sake." She laughed some more and finished with a cough, then flicked the lighter and lit the cigarette without asking if I minded. I smoke, and didn't mind, yet it's nice to be asked.

I'm not the happy homemaker type, but I couldn't stand the spreading, staining puddles. The woman really was a slob, I thought, picking up her raincoat. I hung it on the coat rack, folded her umbrella and stood it in the waste-basket near the door. There was no sign she noticed what I did and no thanks either. Some people should just stay in their own pig pens and not run around spreading their muck.

I headed across the room, intending to get some paper towels from our lounge/storage room to soak up the mess. "As I started to ask a moment ago, is there something I can do, Miss . . . ?"

"Ms. Loudermilk. Voda Beth Loudermilk."

"Ms. Loudermilk, why do you need an investigator?" I paused momentarily in the doorway. Her answer stopped me cold.

"I killed my husband last night. Emptied his own gun into him." The whine was gone, and the words came out in monotone as if she were describing a grocery list. "He died on me." She smashed the cigarette into an ashtray. "Isn't that the silliest thing you ever heard?" She laughed, but sounded close to tears.

If I was surprised because she didn't throw the butt onto the floor, it was only because I was totally wiped out by what she said. I blurted out, "Perhaps you need a lawyer, Mrs. Loudermilk, not a detective."

"It was time *he* hurt some, instead of me."

A quiet even voice interrupted, "Voda Beth. Shut your mouth and keep it shut."

I was so intent, I hadn't noticed someone else had opened the outer door and entered. The speaker was a short wiry man I recognized immediately from his many newspaper photos and television appearances. A shock of steel gray hair, brushed back to emphasize the widow's peak, the piercing blue eyes and every one of his seventy-eight years etched on his face. I'd never met him, of course, but I knew who he was. Hell, everyone knew who "Bulldog" King Porter was—the best criminal lawyer money could buy.

"Oh shit, Bulldog," Voda Beth said. "You know a P.I.'s like a priest. They can't reveal the confidences their clients tell them."

He was dressed like a lawyer would have dressed forty or fifty years ago. Dark charcoal, pinstripe, three-piece suit, white shirt with French cuffs peeking out the prerequisite amount, big gold cufflinks. The tie, a shade lighter than the suit, was not a clip-on and tied with a perfect Windsor knot. A heavy gold link watch chain had a gold Phi Beta Kappa key dangling from one end.

"That only applies to P.I.'s in dime store novels." Bulldog walked over to me and held out his hand. "Ms. Gordon, I've heard a lot about you. I'm Bulldog Porter."

His hand was soft, but the grip firm. "I'm honored to meet you, sir, I've heard a lot about you, too." Porter had begun his practice in Galveston, during the thirties, when the island city considered itself a free state, allowing drinking, gambling and prostitution. He had even defended members of the "beach gang" who smuggled Canadian booze into the Gulf port and shipped it to places like Chicago and Detroit.

"I'll just bet you have, Ms. Gordon." He chuckled. "And let me tell you up front, most of it is true."

Mrs. Loudermilk stood up. Her curly hair framed the sharp angled face which twisted in anger. "Bulldog . . ."

"Voda Beth, just sit right back down there and keep quiet for a minute."

She glared, but did as he said.

"Now, Ms. Gordon . . ."

"Please call me Jenny, Mr. Porter."

"Only if you call me Bulldog."

"Deal. Now, I'm assuming you have a special reason to be here."

"Good. I like that. Cut the crap and right down to brass tacks." He nodded to our storage/lounge area. "Let's go in here and have a little chat. Voda Beth, you stay put." The woman sent him a lethal look, but didn't get up.

"My client in there," he said as we sat at the kitchen-style table, "was mouthing off when I came in. Let's chalk that up to her current emotional state. To her grief, if you will. You see, her husband was shot and killed around 8:00 p.m. last night. She was questioned for hours, eventually charged by the police and locked up in women's detention over at 61 Reisner, just before dawn. She's been without food or sleep for over twenty-four hours."

"Her lack of sleep," I said, "plus the grief and trauma she's experienced, has rendered her incapable of acting correctly or speaking coherently."

"Exactly. I heard you were sharp." He took out a pipe and, within seconds, had asked if I minded and got it lit.

15

Bulldog Porter wasn't known as the plodding, methodical type. "We have great need of an investigator, and you were highly recommended by Lieutenant Hays of HPD homicide department."

The fact Larry Hays sent Porter to me was a surprise. Larry was a good friend, but he still thought it was laughable, my being a private detective. My background is medical; an X-ray technologist. I worked ten years detecting the mystery of the human body and knew nothing about real mysteries. Luckily, C.J. had police experience and I'd been a willing pupil.

If what Bulldog said about the woman was true, she needed help. Maybe I was wrong to condemn her casual attitude about her wet things. If I'd just spent the night in jail, I sure as hell wouldn't be worrying about neatness. Besides, the chance to do a job for Porter was worth considering. G. & G. Investigations wasn't doing so well that we could turn down someone with his clout. "Did she kill her husband?"

He didn't answer immediately. "Voda Beth says she has been physically, sexually and emotionally abused her whole married life. She says he was hitting on her, and she couldn't take it any longer. That she pulled his own gun out from under the mattress and emptied it into him. Her father and I were old school chums, and I agreed to take her case because of him. Actually, it shouldn't be hard to prove diminished capacity." He leaned back, and his eyes zeroed in on mine like an electron beam. "What I need from you, Jenny," he said, smiling, "is to discover if her story of abuse is true."

"Is there any physical evidence of her being beaten, like bruises or anything?"

"Not to my knowledge."

"Has she ever reported to a doctor or to anyone that she was abused?"

16

"I don't think so. But I'd like you to find out."

"What do you know about Mr. Loudermilk?"

"Another thing for you to look into. J. W. Loudermilk owned a development and construction company which was doing quite well until Houston's oil bust. But you'd need to do a thorough background check on him. I do know he was married before, and he has a daughter from that first marriage. The daughter lived with him until recently, and she'd be the first place to start."

"And next, the ex-wife?"

"Precisely. Her name is Elwanda Watson. Had a second marriage which also didn't last. Four children by Watson. I have addresses and phone numbers for you." He set the pipe in the ashtray I'd placed near him, reached into his inner coat pocket and held out an index card. "I believe you've already decided to work for me?"

I smiled as I took the card. "I have indeed." I went to get a copy of our standard contract for his signature. Voda Beth didn't look up when I passed through. When I returned, Porter had written out a check and handed it to me. He'd not inquired about fees. I nearly gasped; it was made out for $5,000.

"I need to have as much information as possible by next Tuesday morning for the preliminary hearing," Bulldog said. "That means working through the weekend if necessary. If you can find out the truth about the Loudermilks' relationship, I might be able to get the charges dropped and we won't have to go to trial."

"If the truth is as she says it is."

"Oh. Naturally. But I believe it is."

Mr. Porter spent a few seconds with our client and left. Then it was time to interview the widow. I walked in and sat behind the desk, searching her face. A neon sign flashing "not guilty" did not appear on her forehead.

"Why don't you tell me what happened, Voda Beth?"

Her eyelids were red-rimmed, and the pale blue eyes were devoid of life or light. She held her body rigid and her mouth tight as if to keep herself from flying apart.

"Look," I said, "I know you're exhausted, and you need food and rest. How about telling me a few brief details, and if I need something else, we can talk later."

She took a deep breath. "J.W. and I had been arguing all evening. If I said black, he said white. I can't remember what started this particular one. Finally, I told him I couldn't take anymore tonight, that I wanted to go to bed. I went to our bedroom and took a shower; he sat in the den and drank."

"Did he drink a lot?"

"Sometimes, and even more lately."

"Why lately?"

"Things were bad financially, really bad the past few months." Voda Beth pressed her hands to her temples, then rubbed them slowly. "I remember now. That's what started the argument. Money. I'd bought two new bras yesterday; the underwire on my last one broke that morning."

My partner C.J. had been a policewoman in Pittsburgh for eight years, and one thing she'd taught me about interviewing someone is it's usually best to not say anything once the person is talking. If you interrupt, you can lose them; they'll clam up.

"I had just finished brushing my hair and was ready to get into bed when J.W. came in, yelling about how stupid I was for spending money we didn't have. He was furious. He sat in there and drank and got madder and madder.

"He got right in my face, screaming, and when I tried to ignore him, he got even madder. He slapped me. Twice at least, and the third time he knocked me onto the bed. He kept hitting with his open hand. One blow made me bite my lip, see?"

She showed me a large blood hematoma inside her cheek. I made appropriate noises of sympathy. "What happened next?"

"He straddled me and started punching me in the stomach and breast with his fists. A blackness came over me, slowly, at first. It got darker and redder. Somehow . . . I really don't know how. I got my hand under the mattress and got hold of his gun. The next thing I knew, he was lying across the bed and . . . and I remembered hearing the gun and there was blood everywhere and . . ."

She began crying, great shuddering sobs. I walked around the desk, handed her a box of Kleenex and patted her shoulder, not really knowing what to say or do. She kept trying to say she didn't mean it, but it was a long time before she got it all out.

When she'd calmed down and blown her nose, I sat down behind the desk. "This wasn't the first time your husband beat you?"

"No. He didn't do it often, and he'd always apologize, say he was sorry and he'd never do it again. That he loved me and didn't want to hurt me." She was back to her monotone voice. "Months would go by, and I'd believe everything was fine, then wham."

"Did you ever tell anyone? Your doctor maybe?"

"No. I was too ashamed. Besides, whatever I'd done to set him off was all my fault. I was the one who . . ."

"Voda Beth. Whatever you did was no reason to be battered or beaten. But my telling you won't help or make any difference to you. You need to get professional help."

"I will. Bulldog is setting it up."

I walked around to her again and patted her shoulder once more. "It's time you went home. You didn't drive over here, did you?"

"Bulldog brought me. He said he'd send someone to pick me up."

"Come on then, I'll go downstairs with you."

A white stretch limo was waiting in the front circular drive when we reached the lobby, and a driver lounging against the front passenger fender saw us and walked over. "Mrs. Loudermilk?" He helped her in, and she waved one finger as he closed the door.

I walked to the parking garage. Lowly private investigators have to drive themselves home.

"If that tight-assed bitch thinks she can kill my father and get away with it, she's crazy."

J. W. Loudermilk's daughter was two months over eighteen, but looked twenty-five. Her name was Elizabeth, but she preferred to be called Liz, she said, after inviting me into her condo in far southwest Houston. She mentioned that she was scheduled for a tennis lesson at the nearby YWCA, but said she could spare a few minutes.

I'd been unable to reach her the evening before and had secretly been glad. Voda Beth's story had unnerved me. With a good night's sleep, I'd hoped to be able to think more rationally. Silly me. My dreams had been filled with a faceless someone who punched and slapped me half the night. It was three o'clock before I finally slid into a dreamless sleep.

I showered and dressed in my weekend office attire—Wrangler jeans and a T-shirt—but since it was a cool forty-nine degrees this morning, I pulled on a sweater. My hair had been short and curly permed for summer, and as I combed through the tangled dark mop, I decided to let it grow for the cooler weather. I checked out a new wrinkle at one corner of my right eye. "Damn Sam. At 33, you shouldn't be having wrinkles," I said. "Someday, you'll have to pay more attention to such things, but not today."

A tiny smudge of cocoa frost eye shadow added depth to my dark eyes, and a quick swipe of powder was easy and fast and completed my bow to cosmetics. Spending time with creams and moisturizers was not my idea of fun, and I intended to fight it as long as possible.

I'd arrived for my appointment with J.W.'s daughter at 10:30 a.m. on the dot.

She had offered a cold drink. I accepted a Diet Coke and sat down as she bustled around in the kitchen. Her living room was a high-beamed ceiling affair, all mirrors, posters and wicker furniture from Pier One Imports. There wasn't a sofa, just two chairs, and a lamp table between them, set before a fireplace. As a young woman out on her own, she probably couldn't afford much.

I studied her as she brought in the drinks. She was lovely, self-assured and poised. She had a heart-shaped face, blue-black hair cut shoulder length and curly permed. Her eyes were such a deep indigo they looked violet, and there was no doubt her resemblance to a young Liz Taylor was often mentioned. She was dressed in a white tennis skirt and top, showing off her golden tan to great advantage. Oh. To be eighteen again, I thought, but only for a brief second.

"Mrs. Gordon?" She seated herself opposite me.

"Jenny, please."

"Okay, Jenny. Let's get one thing cleared up right now. I never did like Voda Beth. She's a coke-snorting, greedy slut who married my father for his money."

21

"You know all this for a fact?" The violet eyes narrowed briefly, before looking at me head-on. Maybe she was sincere, but her clichéd words sounded like the old evil stepmother routine.

"My father owned his own construction and development company. He built office buildings and shopping malls. When his business suffered reverses, she couldn't stand it." Liz sat her glass down on the end table next to her chair, picked up a nail file and began filing her nails. "They argued all the time. Mostly about money. She was always wanting this new dress or that new piece of furniture. Now, with Dad dead, I guess she'll be in high cotton."

"Were their arguments ever violent? Did you see or hear your father hitting her?"

Liz finished the nail she was working on, put that finger to her mouth and began chewing on the cuticle. She shook her head. "Dad did have a temper, but I don't think he ever so much as slapped the bitch."

I sipped on the Diet Coke. "What gives you the idea she'll be in high cotton now? Insurance?"

"She talked him into taking out a policy for two million, a few months ago. She killed him to get that money; there's no doubt in my mind."

I made a mental note to check out the insurance. "How did you find out about this policy?"

"She flaunted it in my face. It's one of those big companies, something Mutual. I'm sure you can find a record of it someplace."

"You mentioned she used coke?"

"I've known ever since I was sixteen and she offered it to me." Liz's face contorted with fury. "That bitch came along and turned my father against me, but it only worked a short time."

"What else did they argue about besides the money?"

"The drugs and the men she slept with."

"She slept around?"

"He said she did. I have no knowledge of that personally."

The picture the girl painted was certainly not something to help Mr. Porter. In fact, it was more likely to hang Voda Beth Loudermilk. But it did strike me strange that the girl didn't have one kind word to say about her stepmother. "How old were you when they married?"

"Thirteen." She drained her glass. "My mother couldn't hold on to Dad. She's a silly bitch, too. Sometimes she doesn't have the sense God gave a goose." She stood. "Sorry, Jenny. I do have to get to the Y for my tennis lesson. My fondest hope is that Voda Beth rots in jail."

Thirteen is a difficult age. I knew from losing my own mother when I was twelve that I would have resented it tremendously if my father had remarried. Her remarks about her own mother seemed strangely out of place though. Didn't this girl like anyone? I wondered. Placing the unfinished Coke on the table, I got up. "Appreciate your talking to me, Liz." I handed her one of my cards. "If you think of anything else I should know, please call."

Liz preceded me to the door and opened it. "If it's something that'll help convict her, you'll hear from me."

It would be easier to make notes of my interview at my office. When I arrived I was surprised to find C.J. at the front desk, hacking away at the computer. "It's good to see you, but weren't you supposed to stay in Dallas all weekend?"

"Yes, but don't ask any questions, okay?" she said and her tone indicated she wasn't kidding. C.J.'s face, which always reminded me of a darker-skinned Nichelle Nichols, the Star Trek actress, was marred by a deep frown of concentration. The new computer we'd recently bought was giving her fits. She continued hitting the buttons and keys like she was working out on a punching bag.

The fun with the football player obviously hadn't worked out. "Ooo . . . kay," I said and told her about our new client, Voda Beth Loudermilk, brought in by Mr. Bulldog Porter himself. She nodded without comment, and I began telling of my interview of Liz Loudermilk. "Liz tried to look and sound sincere, but I'm having a hard time believing her. The hate this girl had was so thick in the room it nearly smothered me."

She paused and turned to listen. "Sounds like she's definitely jealous of the second wife."

"I've tried to imagine how I would feel in that situation. I'm sure I would have resented any woman my father brought in to take my mother's place."

"Five years is a long time to nurse a grudge. Didn't Voda Beth ever do anything nice for Liz?" C.J. looked down at herself and tried to brush off a minute piece of something white from her bright green sweater, gave up and plucked it with her fingernails and tossed it away. The sweater, trimmed in brown and gold leather, was worn over a slim dark brown skirt. She'd added a bright green leather belt, green tinted pantyhose and dark brown boots. At her six foot height, she looked great in whatever she wore, but a couple of years as a model in Manhattan had set her style forever into the high fashion look.

My taste usually runs to Levis or sweats. Of course, no matter what I wore, I still looked just like me, Jenny Gordon, of Houston, Texas. "Liz Loudermilk will cheerfully push the plunger on the syringe if her stepmother is sentenced to die by injection. She ain't too crazy about her own mother, either."

"Maybe she's got a fixation on her father, and anyone else is just a big zero in her mind."

"You're probably right. I was madly in love with my father when I was fourteen," I said, thinking back. "About six months later, I hated him."

"That was a normal growing-up process. I did about the same thing." She smiled and leaned the chair back, folding her hands across her stomach. "Girlfriend, you know what strikes me about your conversation with that girl?"

"That insurance policy?"

"Yes. But besides that. She called Voda Beth a tight-assed bitch. That describes someone uptight or morally rigid. It's not something I normally would associate with a woman who used drugs and slept around."

"You're right. It's total contradiction, isn't it?" I lit a cigarette, forgetting for a moment how much C.J. disliked my smoking.

She fanned the smoke with an exaggerated flip of her black hand. "Get out of here with that thing." She turned back to the computer. "Besides, until I figure out how to trace that insurance policy, I don't need you in my hair." She picked up the telephone receiver. "I guess I'd better call the 'old pro' over at Intertect first and find out where to start."

C.J. had a good working relationship with the private investigators over at Intertect, an office which specialized in computers and databases. Good thing. Computers blow my mind completely. I'd probably never figure this one out.

I went into the lounge and turned on the air purifier and thought about my client. Bulldog Porter had wanted me to find "something" to prove wife abuse. Unfortunately, the talk with Liz Loudermilk had only tightened the noose.

I'd felt sorry for Voda Beth when she told of being beaten. She might even be a greedy slut, but I doubted she was as bad as the girl had tried to make her sound. It's easy to use pop psychology to categorize people, yet the girl did sound like the classic example of a jealous daughter.

I walked through the back office to my desk, taking care not to disturb C.J. as she punched keys on the computer and numbers on the telephone. I called to make a late afternoon appointment with the ex-wife, Elwanda Watson. She worked as a waitress at a seafood restaurant out in the Heights area and said we could meet there. I typed up notes of the "Liz" interview on my old IBM Selectric and placed them in the Loudermilk file. I'd never let that machine go, even if I did learn things like WordPerfect programs and networking with modems.

Just before 5:00 p.m., Elwanda Watson called and changed our meeting to her home. I stacked the paperwork on my desk, told C.J. I'd see her tomorrow, not that she heard me—she was still wrestling with the computer. Just before the door closed, however, she called out, "Sunday brunch at my house, okay?"

Saturday afternoon traffic around the LaGrange Building was thicker than bees around molasses, maddening, but normal. The building is located two and a half blocks from the Galleria. Even in the early fifties, this whole area was still part of a dairy farm. Now, a six-block square area of high dollar shopping malls, department and specialty stores, hotels and high rise office buildings, including developer Gerald Hines' sixty-five story Transco Tower, filled the land where crimson clover used to grow and cows got fat. From the air, the whole area was filled with concrete, steel and bronzed glass and looked like a city skyline, but it's six miles from downtown Houston in suburbia-land. The lack of zoning laws here makes for some unusual building developments.

Elwanda Watson lived in a story-and-a-half house made of white brick and wood and cedar shakes, four miles west of my office. The older neighborhood was built in the late fifties before contractors and architects took a notion to make suburban houses all look alike. These were in a wide range of individual styles and colors. A huge Magnolia tree stood sentinel in front, and a pink bicycle lay on its side in the St. Augustine grass. Four baskets of white and burgundy Impatiens hung from the eaves.

The woman who answered the door was short, overweight, with ponderous breasts and hips almost scraping the doorway. She had short, dark hair streaked heavily with gray and a startled expression which seemed to be a permanent look. She wore a dingy, white sweat suit, no make-up and said she was Elwanda Watson. It would be difficult to believe Liz Loudermilk came from this woman's womb, if it had not been for the eyes. That unique shade of blue, tingeing to violet. Either Elwanda had lost her beauty long ago, or Liz got her looks from her father.

She led me to a large kitchen/den area, both paneled in knotty pine, and there were children's play noises coming from the back yard. She indicated I should sit in the chair across from the sofa and brought tall glasses of iced tea before settling on the Early American style sofa.

I glanced around; the room had the look of having been hastily picked up. A large entertainment cabinet stood against one wall. Wires and plugs stuck out and dangled from the front and one side, indicating sound and electronics had once been installed and then removed. A small TV set was alone on a shelf. Newspapers, magazines, books, and games; Monopoly, Scrabble, Uncle Wiggly, Yahtzee, Parcheesi, Dominoes and cards were piled on and in the cabinet. The drape hung loose from the rod on one side and dragged on the floor. It was an "I don't care look," much like the woman herself. Two failed marriages had taken their toll. "Ms. Gordon, what . . ." she said.

Smiling at her, I said, "Call me Jenny, please."

"And I'm Elwanda. Well, Jenny, what is it you wish to know? This whole horrible thing is too, too weird. Poor old J.W. dead. And Voda Beth accused of killing him. Unbelievable, I tell you. It just boggles my mind."

"It's hard to believe Voda Beth killed J.W.?"

"I'd just never figure her to do something so awful. She seems like such a nice person. Gracious and polite to me, and she's been really kind and generous to my Liz."

"Really? Liz doesn't share your feelings."

"Oh that Liz. She can act like a spoiled brat. The things I could tell you would take half the night. But you don't have time for that. She mouths off about Voda Beth something terrible sometimes, but deep down, I know she likes her step-mom."

"That wasn't the impression I got this morning."

"Oh, I know," said Elwanda. "Liz told me how tacky she was this morning and asked me to apologize for the things she said."

"She doesn't owe me an apology."

"Well, she did mislead you. Made it seem like Voda Beth was a wicked person when she's not." She rubbed both eyes like a person just waking up. "My daughter is beautiful and brilliant, but she can also act like a two-year-old when she doesn't get her way. Sooner or later you have to give in. Of course, she's always sorry afterward and will make up for it a hundred ways."

Despite Elwanda's trying to make Liz sound like nothing more than a rebellious and rambunctious child, I had seen the rage Liz had for Voda Beth. It wasn't just a temper tantrum. I'd hate to see that rage turned on anyone. Elwanda was maternally blind to her child's faults. She didn't want to think otherwise, and I thought it best to get off that subject.

"Voda Beth claimed J.W. was beating her when she killed him. Was he ever abusive to you?"

"Oh, my. No. I was married to the man for ten years, and he never raised a hand to me." She looked directly at me, and her wide-eyed look of astonishment was more pronounced. "And I don't see him abusing Voda Beth, either. He worshipped her. He was always a kind and wonderful husband. And father. Always."

If that was true, I wondered, then why did she divorce this Boy Scout? I had to ask. "Why did you . . ."

"Divorce him? He left me. For another woman. Not Voda Beth; it was over long before he met her. There were lots of other women. Some men are born womanizers, and J.W. was one. That is, until Voda Beth caught him. I don't think he ever strayed from her." Tears welled up in those big violet eyes and, this overweight, throw-away wife's voice held a wistful note.

"What about his low boiling point?"

It took her a moment to speak. "He could get angry, real easy-like when he was young, but he'd mellowed out. Even so, his anger never, ever, led to violence."

"Did Voda Beth ever go out on him?"

"I don't think so. He probably would've told me if she had."

I raised an eyebrow.

"It's sounds funny, I guess, but after he married her, he

and I got real friendly-like. I mean, like close friends. He apologized for hurting me in the past. He was so good when my marriage with Don Watson broke up. Offered me money because he knew I was having a hard time with four little kids."

At their mention, the children's voices outside reached a crescendo, and she walked to the patio door to check. Evidently, it was nothing which needed her presence. Mother-like, however, she stuck her head out and told them to stop whatever they were doing and find something else to do. She came back to the sofa and sat. "I think it was because he was finally happy. He said once, Voda Beth had taught him the right way to treat a woman and he'd learned his lesson."

Obviously, Elwanda still had deep feelings for J.W. Loudermilk, and she wasn't going to say anything against him. Unfortunately, what she said was detrimental to my client. If J.W. didn't have a history of abusing women, it looked like Voda Beth had lied. I stood. "I appreciate your talking to me."

"Sorry I wasn't more help." We headed to the front door and she said, "Oh, I just thought of something. It's possible they had some fights over Liz. That was one thing he could get angry enough to come to blows over. Although, I still don't see it."

"Why not?"

"Liz would have told me about it."

After the way the girl had talked about her mother, I was not sure she'd confide in Elwanda, but what do I know about daughters? Especially teen-age ones.

"Liz was very angry with her father the past few years— for breaking up our marriage, for marrying Voda Beth. For what she saw as him neglecting her. She would gripe and complain how he didn't pay any attention to her, how he was always fawning over Voda Beth. Now that I think on it, she must have been jealous of her father."

That could explain the rage I saw in the girl. "I guess that's normal in young girls who want their father all to themselves."

"She could get all worked up about it. Throw fits and scream at him. That's one reason he made her move out of the house."

"He made his own daughter leave?"

"About three months ago. She was working and making good money, but she would stay out all hours and do things to aggravate him—like smoking pot in the house. Anyway, he got fed up. Although Voda Beth tried to stop him, he made Liz get a place of her own. She was really bent all out of shape over that for awhile."

"I guess it's hard to be a parent these days." I thanked her again and left.

I headed back to my apartment, grateful the traffic had slacked off. It gave me time to wonder about my client. Whatever had happened that night in the Loudermilks' home was still muddled, but it looked as if my client had lied through her teeth.

I ate a light dinner, grilled chicken and a big salad and spent the rest of the evening reading a P.I. novel.

I went to bed, and just before drifting off to sleep, I decided tomorrow I'd call Lieutenant Larry Hays of Houston's homicide department. Maybe the police and autopsy reports would give me some fresh insights.

I called Larry Hays on his car phone and caught him as he was driving away from headquarters to go have breakfast. "No rest for the wicked, huh?"

"Not on Sunday," he said. "Meet me at Kay's in twenty minutes."

Kay's was a favorite hangout of law enforcement personnel. The restaurant's owner, Bert DeLeon, had a thing about listening to the cop's war stories. He really got into that stuff. He'd been especially fond of my late husband, and when Tommy introduced me to him, I figured if Bert had not approved, Tommy would not have proposed. Kay's served family style food and gave better service than the high priced restaurants.

Lieutenant Hays sat at the back booth on the west side and a mug of coffee was waiting for me. "Are you eating?" he asked.

"Just an English muffin and half a grapefruit."

"Watching your weight again?"

"Always. I weighed 125 this morning."

"That's about your normal, isn't it?"

"Yes, but you know how I love chicken-fried steak and Mexican food. The only way I can indulge is to keep this five-feet-six-inch woman on that 125."

"Poor baby."

Larry is six-three and weighs about 185 and never has to watch his weight because he has a great metabolism. It was frustrating, and I tried not to think about it. "Just shut up and eat your cholesterol-filled eggs and pancakes and bacon."

"I intend to."

Larry had been my husband's partner and friend from the day they were rookies, until politics had caused Tommy to resign and become a private detective. Larry took on a self-appointed task of watching out for me after my husband was killed, and sometimes it was stifling. We'd had several arguments about it, but recently he had weakened.

Mostly because I'd learned from C.J. how to handle myself. He was a damn good cop, and I respected his opinions. It was easier when he respected mine.

After we'd eaten, he answered my questions about the Loudermilk case. "The medical examiner has some doubts about your client's story."

"What?"

"The angle of the shot for one thing. Mrs. Loudermilk says she was crouched on the bed when she shot him, but that doesn't wash. The M.E. says the shooter was standing. If she were as close to him as she says there would have been powder burns on his body. The M.E. says the shooter had to be standing, at least twelve to fourteen feet away."

"Wow. Bulldog's not going to like that."

Larry ran a big hand through his sandy hair. "Probably a good thing. I don't think he can prove she was abused."

"Why not?"

"I talked to our police psychologist, and although he didn't talk to her, he says she doesn't display the attitude of a battered woman. Immediately after a battering, most women usually act meek and acquiescent. She came in there full of self-confidence. Almost daring us to believe her." Larry signaled the waitress to bring him more coffee. "She's got all the buzz words and phrases down pat. Like how he got boozed up and how he used his open hand on her face and his fists on her breasts and abdomen."

"Yeah, she gave me those classic statements, too, the ones I've read about; like how he'd say he was sorry and how she deserved it."

His hazel eyes narrowed. "At one point Thursday night, the sex crimes unit took her over to get a medical exam. No evidence of sexual intercourse. They noticed a couple of bruises on her torso, but thought they could have been self-inflicted. She gave us a pretty good story, but she hasn't given us the truth yet."

"Could she be covering for someone. Like maybe the daughter?"

"Possibly, but the captain and the D.A. want to go ahead with the indictment, anyway. The physical evidence and her confession wraps everything up in a nice neat package with a big bow. I just never have liked neat packages."

"The daughter is seething with rage against the step-mother."

"Rage isn't evidence. Lots of daughters hate their step-parents. You don't have to worry. Bulldog will plead Voda Beth on diminished capacity and get her off, or he'll plea bargain." He absently stirred the coffee and then realized he hadn't added the sugar yet. "I do have a funny feeling there's something else."

"I guess I'd better talk to Bulldog. He's not going to be too happy with this."

"Likely not." He grabbed the check and stood. "I hate to eat and run," he said, "but I've got to go interrogate witnesses in a drive-by shooting last night."

"Have fun."

"Oh, yeah," he said harshly, his mind already to the task that lay ahead.

I headed for the office and, for once, the traffic wasn't a problem. Sunday morning is one of the rare good times to drive in this congested Bayou city.

I had talked with C.J. before leaving home and canceled our brunch date. She said she'd go to the office and see what she could turn up on the computer. She wanted to run credit records on all three women, Voda Beth and Liz Loudermilk and Elwanda Watson; and throw in J. W. Loudermilk, too.

She'd made coffee. I poured a cup and sat down next to her desk. She had not found anything unusual on the women's credit records, and the daughter hadn't established any credit yet. We discussed my interview with Elwanda, and I told her what Larry had said. "I'd better call Bulldog. I don't have one solitary thing to help him. He'll probably want to fire us."

"Okay," she said, "but I've got a couple more checks to make while you're getting us fired."

I walked back to my desk and called Bulldog Porter's office. His answering service said he'd call me back within the hour, or if he didn't, for me to call again.

Twenty minutes later, C.J. came in my office, a gleam in her dark eyes. "I got it."

"What?" I asked, not remembering what she'd been trying to do. I was still waiting on Bulldog to return my call and was trying to get my reports ready for him and figure out how much I could deduct from the $5,000 he had given me.

"Remember Liz Loudermilk told you about a big insurance policy?" I nodded. "She was right. You're going to love this."

"Uh-oh. Don't tell me you've found another motive for Voda Beth."

"Our client isn't the only one with a motive. Little Miss Liz could inherit it all. All by herself."

"Oh, yeah? How?"

"If Voda Beth dies first or is disqualified, it all goes to the loving daughter."

"All..ll rii..ii..ght. And I guess if ole Voda Beth goes to prison for killing her husband, she'll be disqualified?"

"You got that right, Ms. Gordon, and to help put Liz to the top of the suspect list—you won't believe this—she put money down yesterday on a brand new, fiery red Miata."

"You have got to be kidding."

"If I'm lying, I'm dying. But just don't forget one important thing—stepmommy's told you and the police a big lie."

"That's okay. Old Bulldog will say she made that statement under duress," I said. "This is just what he needed. It gives him some ammunition for his reasonable doubt."

"Wonder what the lovely Liz was doing that night?"

I called Lieutenant Hays, knowing he'd need to know what we'd found. Luckily, he was near his car phone, and I filled him in on Liz. He wasn't too happy. The case was closed as far as he was concerned, but after he grumbled, he said he'd talk with the daughter tomorrow to see if she had an alibi for the night in question.

"C.J., I think Liz did it and our client confessed, all under some misguided idea to protect Liz. Bulldog can take this and run with it."

"When do I get to meet this mouthpiece anyway?"

"Anytime you say. You'll like him; he's positively charming."

"Unh-unh. No way I'm gonna like a shyster who useta work fo' de mob. Those guys ain't nobody for this li'l black girl to mess wid'."

As usual, her slipping into southern black, street talk cracked me up. Coming from such a smart and beautiful woman it was funny.

As I laughed, she said, "By the way, while running those credit card histories, I did find a few interesting tidbits on old J.W. himself."

"How can someone who sounds like you be so smart? You can check credit card records?"

"If you know the right buttons to push and Intertect does." She handed me the printout of J. W. Loudermilk's

Visa and American Express statements for the past year.

I flipped through them. "Holy shit, this is scary. You don't expect any old Jane Blow to be able to run a credit card account check."

"Oh hell," she said, her voice full of pride, "not just any old Jane Blow can do it. It takes a few brains and persistence. I took what I learned from my investigator pals and played around for awhile and was able to come up with a password for a security code."

"My partner—the smartass computer hack." I was scanning the account statements and something caught my attention. Loudermilk had visited three different doctors in the past month and had charged his visits to his Amex. "Wonder what this medical stuff is all about?"

"Give that girl a gold star. That's what I thought was so interesting."

"I happen to know this Doctor Gaudet is a neurosurgeon. I'm not sure about the other two."

"Think I should check them out?" She grinned.

"Holy shit. Why didn't I think of that."

"Because you hired me to think for you."

"Someone has to do the important stuff," I said. "I don't want to talk to Voda Beth again. It makes me mad when a client lies to me, but I could go talk to Elwanda Watson again. Maybe J.W. confided some medical problem to her. It's probably not important though."

"Fine. But do it tomorrow. I make a motion we get out of here. Sunday's almost over, and we need a little R & R."

"Honey," I said, using one of her favorite expressions, "you ain't never lied."

Monday morning dawned with Houston shrouded in fog. Not unusual this time of year; with cooler air sweeping down across Texas and meeting the warm Gulf air, it was inevitable. It looked like the sun would burn it off around ten, and sure enough, I was right. When I left for Elwanda's around 10:30, there were only a few pockets of misty stuff, although the sky was still hazy.

I had not called first for an appointment; sometimes it's better to catch people when they're not on guard. Turns out Elwanda was not the only one to be surprised. I found my client, Voda Beth Loudermilk, visiting Elwanda. Neither seemed pleased to see me, but I didn't let that stop me. They were both dressed in gowns and robes, but it looked as if neither had slept. What was going on between these two? I wondered.

They sat on the sofa next to each other, and I sat in a platform rocker which angled off to their right. After exchanging a few politenesses, I mentioned homicide was interviewing Liz this morning, setting off quite a reaction.

Voda Beth practically yelled at me. "Liz didn't have anything to do with anything. I'm the one who shot J.W. The police already have my statement." She burst out crying, and Elwanda moved closer to put her arms around Voda Beth, making soothing sounds as if comforting a baby.

"I resent someone accusing my daughter," Elwanda said. "Was that your idea, Ms. Gordon?"

"Not exactly. But some new information about Liz did come to my attention. Naturally, I had to tell the lieutenant in charge."

"What information?" she asked.

"I'm not at liberty to say."

Voda Beth was crying so hard, she began coughing, and Elwanda got up to get a glass of water. As she moved to the kitchen, the telephone rang. The receiver was a few feet from her, but when she shot a quick look at Voda Beth, she turned and said, "Jenny, would you mind getting that?"

I walked into the kitchen as Elwanda hurried back to the sofa. "Watson's residence," I said.

"Jenny, is that you? Good. I thought you should know what I found out from Doctor James Gaudet. Seems that Loudermilk had a deep-seated, inoperable brain tumor."

I turned my back to the two women and kept my voice low. "Neuroblastoma?"

"Some big long name," she said. "I'm not sure if that was it, but the doctor said it was bad. Real bad. That he'd never seen a malignancy grow so fast. The man was only weeks away from blindness, paralysis and death."

"Sound like Loudermilk's luck . . . wait a minute."

"Now. Now, you're thinking. This may have been planned."

"A mercy killing . . . maybe."

"Bingo. Something else you should know. Larry called. Liz has a strong alibi. She and a girlfriend were babysitting for her younger brothers and sisters at her mom's house."

"Where did Elwanda go?"

"Liz says she doesn't know, but maybe . . ."

"The Loudermilks'," C.J. and I said in unison. I thought for a moment, then said, "Why don't you call Bulldog Porter? Ask him to come over here immediately. This may get interesting." I hung up the receiver, walked to the coffee pot and poured a cup, but it was bitter.

I could see Elwanda and Voda Beth still huddled. It looked as if both had been crying, but there were signs of recovery. I rinsed out the coffee pot. The coffee canister was empty, and it took me a few minutes to locate a new can, open it and get the pot dripping. I'd just poured three cups when the front doorbell rang.

Elwanda answered it and led Bulldog back into the den.

Both women were definitely not expecting him and wanted to know what was going on. Would someone please tell them?

I handed the coffee around and then stood near the glass patio door and began. "I'm presenting a hypothetical case here, Bulldog. If you ladies will, please listen." They turned tear-streaked faces to me. Elwanda's permanent look of astonishment was more pronounced. Voda Beth looked tired. Bone tired.

"I think there was this nice man, who had a nice wife and a nice ex-wife and a not-so-very-nice brain tumor. He knows he doesn't have much time before he will be totally incapacitated and a short time after that, he will die. He doesn't want to die like that. The man also had some business losses. There's the wife and an eighteen-year-old daughter to think about." You could have heard an eye blink, they were so quiet.

"I think this very nice man decided to commit suicide. Everything is planned, but that night for some reason, maybe fear, he was unable to do this alone. He asked his wife for help. She refused. He was on somewhat friendly terms with his ex-wife, and he calls her. The ex comes over. He convinces the women time is running out. That the job must be done. The discussion continues, he is adamant, he begs and cajoles and one of them is convinced to help. Maybe it was the ex. But the wife says to the ex-wife, no, if anything goes wrong what will happen to your children? You can't go to prison. I won't allow it. But I can't kill the man I love, either. Finally, one woman does it, and the wife calls the police."

I looked at each woman, was unable to read the truth. "How does that sound to you ladies? Bulldog?"

No one said anything, but I saw big tears running, first

down Voda Beth's face and then, Elwanda's. Silent tears which quietly dripped into their laps, leaving traces on the robes. Their hands were clasped tightly together.

Elwanda said, "That's pretty much what happened. I'm the one who shot him first. Voda Beth took the gun then and emptied it into him, so if the police tested her hands there would be gun powder traces and her fingerprints would be on the gun."

"No." The anguish was clear and strong in Voda Beth's voice. "I'm the one who fired the gun. She had nothing to do with it. I killed him, and I'll take the punishment."

"Bulldog," I said. "Looks like you've got your hands full."

"Oh no," he said, "this one is already won. I doubt there will even be a trial. And if there is, plea bargaining is still an option. Thank you for your help, Jenny. You can expect business from me, now and then, when I have the need of an investigator. Send me an invoice for your expenses."

I walked sadly out of Elwanda Watson's house and drove to the LaGrange, parked and walked inside. When I reached our office, C.J. asked, "Which one did it? Who fired the gun?"

"I don't think it really matters. They just did what they thought had to be done."

Arsenic and Old Ideas

I

Robbie Dunlap had a feeling she should stay home and miss her writers' meeting, but she couldn't put her finger on exactly why. It wasn't a premonition. It was only a vague uneasiness and had more to do with the fact her husband, Damon, the Sheriff of Adobe County, was going on a raid with some Austin law officers. She always felt tense when Damon had to be out in the boonies, kicking doors open to search for bad guys.

Frontier City, the county seat of Adobe County, was small; crime usually ran to misdemeanors. But the county's rugged limestone and granite hills and small canyons made good hiding places for criminals and their activities. Located one mile off Interstate-35, the town was forty minutes northwest of Austin, Texas, and a mere one hundred thirty miles southwest of the Ft. Worth-Dallas metroplex, making it highly accessible to the bad guys. Tonight's raid was to round up a gang suspected of truck hijacking.

Robbie didn't worry much about Damon; at four inches above six feet tall and two hundred thirty-eight pounds, he was capable of taking care of himself. It was just—well, she didn't know exactly what it was. She pushed her uneasy thoughts aside and continued loading the dishwasher.

Robbie Dunlap was fifty-five years old, in her prime, she thought on her better days. Their two children were grown and on their own.

Robbie was glad to have the mother things over with so

she could do what she had always wanted—write mystery books. She had worked at the Adobe County hospital for twenty years as an X-ray technologist, and now she wanted to fulfill her dreams.

Her K.P. duty was completed when Damon walked into the kitchen and asked, "Honey, where's my new belt?"

"I hung it in your closet on your belt rack."

"Well, I can't find it."

"I'll swear you can't find your behind with both hands, Damon." After twenty-nine and a half years, they shared the easygoing banter of longtime companions. "If you don't get your eyes checked, I'm buying you a seeing-eye dog for Christmas."

"I'd be happy to get my eyes checked if you'll tell me where I'm getting the money to pay for it." The Adobe County sheriff's pay wasn't the greatest, and without her income they often had to struggle.

Damon groped for her backside as she walked past him. "I can still find *your* behind even if I can't see."

She laughingly pushed at his hand. "That's fine. Being half blind makes it harder for you to see my wrinkles and gray hair."

"Wallowing in self-pity because you're menopausal?"

"Don't mess with me. Besides, I have more important things on my mind than my body changes."

"Like your writers' meeting tonight? Worried about your chapter?" Damon was pleased Robbie was writing and encouraged her. Their only conflict came when she wanted to nose around in his cases for "research." Damon felt "police business was police business" and a civilian—especially a wife—should stay out of it.

"Yes, maybe a little, but I'm . . ." She bit her lip, not wanting to tell him of her uneasiness. Instead she got the new belt and handed it to Damon, who was standing just inside the bedroom door. "If it had been a snake, Damon, it would have bitten you. It was right there on the belt rack, like I told you."

"But then I wouldn't have got you into the bedroom, would I?" He threw the belt across the bed and took her in his arms. "I know, we're both in a hurry, but don't we have time for one little kiss?"

"You'd better have, old man," she said, kissing him, "or I might look around for a young stud to keep company with—one who can see."

"What would you do with him? Spend all your time training him?" Damon released her, picked up the belt, slid it through the loops on his Levis, and attached his holster and gun. "Don't worry about me, hon. I'll let those city boys pop that door, and I'll wait until they've secured the house before I go in. About all a blind man can do, anyway."

"Ha. I know you, Sheriff Dunlap. You'll be right there up front. Besides, you don't want those city slickers thinking you're a cowardly old lion. Just remember your flak jacket."

They walked back to the living room, arms around each other, and Damon asked, "What time is your meeting over?"

"Nine-thirty to ten, as usual."

"Meeting at Mary Lou's office—right?"

"Ummm," she said and handed him a thermos of coffee.

"I'll be back whenever," he said and gave her another quick kiss before walking out the back door.

Ten minutes later, Robbie drove the six blocks into downtown Frontier City. As in many Texas county seats built around the turn of the century, the county courthouse

44

sat in the center of town. Businesses ringed the courthouse square. A flower shop, two restaurants, an insurance office, a dry cleaner's, a drugstore, a card and gift shop, two dress shops, a jewelry store, a movie theater, and a Sears catalog store were on three sides; a hotel with a coffee shop and a bank made up the fourth side.

Economic times had hit hard in the late 1980s, but because of the natural lake west of town, excellent schools, and a lower tax rate, new growth had begun. People from Austin were lured in record numbers as they scurried from the stress-filled city to the ease of small town life.

Robbie drove one block south of the courthouse square and parked next door to the one-story building that housed MacLean's Real Estate office, where their meetings were held every other Thursday. It was six forty-five p.m. Everyone tried to be on time and start promptly at seven.

II

Lilabeth Watson, the group's youngest member at age thirty—painfully shy, with a fragile ego Robbie tried to mother along—began reading: "Caladonia Jones gave the nod to her lead guitarist to begin the final song of the evening, opened her mouth, and her band kicked in, right on cue.

Ah-ah-maz-zi-ing Grace, ho-ow sweet the sound . . .

Tha-at saved a-a-a wretch li-ike me-e . . ."

Robbie said, "Wait. Are you going to include the whole first stanza of the song?"

"Well, yes . . ." said Lilabeth. "I think so."

"That might slow it too much there. How about just the first line?"

"I agree," said Winona Baldwin, her voice barely concealing her impatience. Winona had wanted to read first, but Lilabeth said she had to because little Adam was running a slight fever and Bob always got so nervous. Winona gave in, but had rolled her eyes.

Winona Baldwin was even more shy about her work than Lilabeth, especially when it came to reading out loud. She'd just recently gained some confidence, but only when her sister-in-law wasn't around.

There were four regulars in the Thursday night writing group, but sometimes a fifth member came, Arlene Saunders. Arlene and Winona were sisters-in-law. Winona's husband, Eric, and Arlene were brother and sister.

Tonight everyone planned to read her first chapter to insure their openings were intriguing and fast paced, to double check that everyone had a hook—that sometimes elusive, unputdownable magic that keeps readers and editors turning pages.

Robbie was secretly glad Arlene Saunders had not shown up tonight. Arlene didn't want to write as much as she wanted to talk about writing. The woman also had a way of giving a scathing critique without knowing what she was talking about. That was devastating. Especially for Winona and Lilabeth.

The five women planned to enter their manuscripts in the River City Mystery Association's First Novel Contest, and the deadline was January 1st, only thirteen weeks away. The winner would win a $15,000 advance and publication of her book.

Lilabeth was writing a romantic suspense featuring a country and western singer; Winona, a psychological thriller; and Mary Lou's was a cozy. Robbie's own entry featured a husband and wife who owned a detective agency.

The absent Arlene's was about a woman in jeopardy, although no one had ever seen anything in writing.

Robbie was the only one in the group who'd ever been published and paid for it—two mystery short stories in *Ellery Queen* magazine. She wanted to win the first prize and be published. She also wanted that prize money.

When Lilabeth finished reading, Winona Baldwin got up for her turn. After clearing her throat excessively, Winona read. Nothing was said as she finished, but in a moment Lilabeth stammered, "I-I like it. Your characters are excellent and everything works well, but . . ." She paused and looked at the others. Lilabeth didn't like to give an opinion entirely on her own.

"The opening was definitely boring," said Mary Lou. When Lilabeth and Robbie agreed with her, Winona's face twisted and tears came into her eyes.

Mary Lou said, "Winona, don't get upset. You've got it. That second chapter you read last week is the beginning. That's where your story really starts."

Winona's tears were threatening to spill. "Oh, great." She gathered up the pages and held them in one hand while she slapped on them with her other hand. "I've rewritten this until I'm blue in the face. Now y'all say I have to do another stupid rewrite."

Robbie tried to placate Winona. "No, you don't have to change a word or sentence. Just start with chapter two and feed the narrative from chapter one into the second and third chapters."

Lilabeth said, "It's all on computer; it'll only take an hour or so."

"Easy for you to say." Winona's voice got argumentative. "Do you know what I have to go through to use Eric's computer?" She threw the manuscript across the room, and the pages scattered all over the floor.

"Winona, getting angry doesn't help," Robbie said, although she'd rather see a little anger than Pitiful Patty tears.

"Eric's feeling bad—vomiting—some kind of intestinal flu, and that means he'll be home all week, griping and complaining. Especially about me touching his precious computer." She sniffled. "If he's home he won't let me use his computer because he needs it, he says. And if I use it when he's gone, he bitches and says I always mess up his stuff somehow. I might as well give up writing. It's just not worth it."

Robbie knew Eric resented Winona's writing. "Okay, just copy everything onto a floppy. Next week, when he's gone again, you can come to my house and work."

"You mean it?"

Robbie nodded and got up to help Winona pick up the papers.

When they finished, Winona said, "I'd better get on home now. Eric will be mad if I'm late." Winona stuffed her manuscript into a grocery sack and, without waiting for the others to read, walked out the back door.

"Gosh," said Lilabeth. "Is she just touchy tonight or what?"

"She gets uptight when Eric's in town, and if he's sick, I'm sure things are worse," said Robbie.

Mary Lou snorted. "I doubt Eric's sick. He's probably on dope."

"Really?" asked Lilabeth, her eyes growing big and round with the news. For a thirty-year-old she was still quite naive.

Mary Lou said, "He's abused alcohol for years. Drug abuse wouldn't surprise me." Mary Lou glanced at her watch, took her own manuscript out of her briefcase, and set it on the desktop. "We'll just have to forget about the trials and tribulations of Eric and Winona Baldwin. Else we'll never get through." She glanced at Robbie and raised an eyebrow. "Do you want to read next?"

Robbie was glad Mary Lou had changed the subject back to their writing. She didn't want to get into idle gossip about the Baldwins. It made her too angry. She had seen Winona's bruises and knew the real story behind the cracked ribs and broken arm. But what made her even more angry was that Winona stayed and put up with Eric's brutality.

"You go ahead," said Robbie. "My first chapter is only five pages."

Mary Lou said, "Good. Maybe we'll get home early tonight." She read her title: "A Pforensics Pfable Pfrom Pflugerville by Mary Lou MacLean."

Robbie had to cough and fake a sneeze to hide her dismay at the cutesy title. She did, however, understand Mary Lou's brand of madness. The woman had grown up in the town of Pflugerville, where her father was still an undertaker, and Mary Lou was an unabashed fan of Charlotte MacLeod. Anytime she could emulate Ms. MacLeod, she didn't hesitate.

Mary Lou continued: "Victoria Gladstone had just finished wiping the blood up from her previously spotless kitchen floor, washed her hands, and fluffed her hair when the doorbell rang."

Someone began a loud knocking on the door of the real estate office. Mary Lou stopped. "Lilabeth, you're closest . . ."

Robbie spoke up. "Ask who it is first, okay?"

Lilabeth went to the door. "Who is it?"

"Damon Dunlap. Is my wife there?"

Lilabeth unlocked the door, and Damon stepped into the doorway and greeted them with a grim-faced hello.

Robbie walked over to the door. "Are the kids all okay?" and followed when he indicated he wanted her to step outside.

"The kids are fine. Is Winona Baldwin here? I didn't see her car."

"She left a few minutes ago." Robbie felt her stomach lurch and her uneasiness returned. "What's wrong?"

"Eric Baldwin is dead."

"Eric is wha . . . ? My Lord, what happened?"

"We don't know yet. His sister, Arlene, went by the house. Said she'd talked to him a little earlier, and he said he was sick—really bad sick. When she drove out there, the garage door was open and a light was on inside. Arlene found his body on the ground next to his car."

"How horrible. Oh, heavens, Winona's going home to . . ."

"My deputies are out there, but I'd hoped to break the news myself. How long did you say she's been gone?"

"I didn't, but probably not more than fifteen to twenty minutes."

"What time did she get here?"

"She and Lilabeth were last. They came one behind the other. About three minutes to seven. Why do you want to know?"

"And exactly when did she leave?"

Robbie saw it was now nine-thirty. "Probably a little after nine. She'd mentioned Eric was sick. How did he . . . ?"

"I can't tell you what it is, but there is strong evidence of foul play."

"Why are you asking all this about Winona?"

"You know the old cop's adage about checking out the spouse."

"Oh, Damon, surely you don't think Winona could have . . . I can't believe Winona . . ." Robbie's voice trailed off as she remembered Eric's harsh treatment of his wife.

"It's just routine to establish an alibi," said Damon. "Not that she's given me one yet. I'd better get back to their farm."

Robbie went back inside and told the others Eric Baldwin had died, but that she didn't have any details.

"Poor Winona," said Lilabeth.

"Poor Winona, my foot," said Mary Lou. "It's the best thing that ever happened to her."

"Mary Lou, don't. I know you don't mean it." Robbie stopped her friend. She had been thinking the same thoughts, but her worry that somehow Winona was involved made her want to keep Mary Lou from starting gossip.

"I'm only being truthful. Eric Baldwin was not a pleasant man. It's no secret he made Winona's life miserable. I wouldn't be surprised . . ."

How had Mary Lou come up with the idea? All she'd told them was what she knew—that Eric Baldwin was dead. She had to get Mary Lou's mind sidetracked. "Look, we'd better call it a night. I can't concentrate now, and besides, Winona will need help tomorrow. By the time the families get here there'll be lots of mouths to feed."

The others agreed, and they all went home.

Robbie tried to stay awake until Damon returned, but dozed. When he got home, Damon didn't know much more. They'd have to wait until an autopsy was done to determine the exact cause of death. He took a quick shower and climbed into bed beside Robbie.

She was nearly asleep again, but roused up to ask him what happened on the Austin police raid.

"It was postponed."

"Why?" Robbie asked and stifled a yawn.

"The Fed's informant called and said if we waited until Sunday night, the barn would be full of stolen merchandise."

"Oh." Robbie yawned again.

"I'm sorry, you have three more days to worry."

"Worry?" she mumbled. " 'Bout an old blind man?"

"Maybe only because you love this old man?" Damon asked.

But Robbie didn't answer. She'd fallen asleep.

III

"Arlene Saunders says Winona told her more than once she'd get even with Eric someday," Damon said. "Get even for all those beatings."

Damon would carefully edit his answers, omitting police evidence, but he'd answer most questions when she asked for details. Robbie thought talking to her helped him to clarify his thinking. "I'm sure she was just mouthing off, like anyone would. Winona didn't kill him. I feel it in my bones."

"Well, somebody sure did. Doc Timmons says Eric Baldwin has traces of arsenic in his digestive tract. He'll know for sure when he gets the lab results, but he's ninety percent sure it was rat poison." Damon took another bite of his luncheon salad. "Winona admitted last night how afraid she was of Eric."

"I'm sure she was. I don't think anyone who knew her

would doubt it, but if she was so afraid, how could she have the nerve to kill him?"

"It doesn't take much nerve to put rat poison in somebody's food, and I'm afraid the method puts Winona at the top of the list. Women have a history of using poison . . ."

Robbie sighed in exasperation. "Oh, you chauvinist, you only remember Arsenic and Old Lace. I remember doing some library research for one of my stories and reading about poison. Historically more men than women have used poison to kill. They've been doing it for hundreds of years."

"Well, if you have a better suspect, why don't you tell me. Winona had motive, opportunity, and means. The arsenic was conveniently in Eric's garage."

"Where almost anyone else had access to it." Robbie got up to refill their iced tea glasses.

"But who else had a motive?"

"I don't know. Let me think about it."

"Robbie, you'd better stay out of this. This involves one of your friends, and she just might turn out guilty. This is real life honey, not mystery fiction." Damon smiled to show her he wasn't mad, but she also knew the question time was over. "I'm going to be late if I don't leave now." He did stay long enough to drink half of his iced tea and kiss the top of Robbie's head before he left.

Robbie cleared the table and rinsed the dishes. Her writing group—Winona, Mary Lou, Lilabeth, and herself—shared a kinship, a sisterhood even; none of them was capable of killing except on paper. She somehow had to steer Damon to another motive or suspect.

Before noon Robbie had made a potato casserole to take to the Baldwin house, and when the kitchen was clean from lunch, she got out the ingredients to make pecan pies. She wanted to have everything ready to deliver by three.

Robbie rolled the pie crust and thought about murder. If Winona wasn't guilty, then who? Only two other people, Arlene and J. T. Saunders, were close to Eric and Winona. Robbie didn't care for Arlene, but the woman hero-worshiped her brother and probably wouldn't kill him. That left her husband, J.T., or someone unknown.

She didn't know if J.T. was capable of murder; she barely knew him. But what motive could he have? Robbie couldn't think of anything.

A business associate or coworker of Eric's maybe? Could someone there have a reason to want Eric dead? She knew practically nothing about his work.

Eric Baldwin had traveled the southwest selling farm equipment for years, but had been laid off two years ago. Winona said he'd found another sales job, and he went out of town regularly, but Robbie didn't know what he sold these days. She'd ask Winona about Eric's work when she made her bereavement call with the food. A real motive was what Damon needed.

Robbie dreaded seeing Winona; the death of a hus-band—even a brute—wouldn't be easy. And the Baldwin children's grief would be heart-wrenching.

To Robbie's knowledge, Eric had never abused his chil-dren, but she had worried it would happen one day. Now he would never have the chance to harm them, and she couldn't help being relieved about that.

Most of all she dreaded talking to Arlene, the quasi member, of their writing group. Her jealousy had caused her to become bitter and vituperous. But Arlene had only herself to blame. They wrote, and she didn't.

The Baldwin farm was five miles south of Frontier City. Robbie drove out and turned into a long gravel driveway that led to a garage and continued on to a huge barn in the back. Up next to the house, the driveway had been paved and widened enough to accommodate several cars. An old Plymouth, an RV, and two pickup trucks were parked there today. Robbie pulled up next to the pickup she recognized as belonging to Arlene's husband, J. T. Saunders. She noticed the yellow crime-scene tape across the garage door as she got out and looked around. She was surprised at the signs of neglect she saw.

She remembered when Winona and Eric had bought the old two-story house ten years ago. It had originally been built and owned by one of Eric's ancestors. A huge front porch wrapped around to one side—good for catching an evening breeze in the days before air-conditioning. Winona had once been excited about restoring it.

Now paint peeled from the wood and a streak—the color of old blood—ran down from a corner rain gutter. Portions of the weather-beaten porch sagged. The refurbishing dreams had crumbled along with the job and the marriage, Robbie thought.

Five or six children of indeterminate ages were throwing a volleyball around on the sparse front lawn. As Robbie waved to Winona's two, she noticed Arlene standing at the side entrance holding open a screen door.

Arlene helped bring in the food, and Robbie asked about Winona. Arlene said Winona was lying down, that the doctor had given her some tranquilizers. Once inside, the two women walked down a short hallway to the kitchen. Several people wandered in and out of the kitchen, and Arlene introduced them. Some were Eric's relatives, and some were Winona's.

"How are you holding up, Arlene?"

Arlene was putting the casserole Robbie brought into the icebox. She turned, and Robbie could see her eyes were red rimmed. "I'm doing okay. It was hard this morning when I went with Winona to make funeral arrangements." She sniffed. "How about some coffee or iced tea?" Robbie said tea would be fine, and they sat at the kitchen table.

J. T. Saunders suddenly came in through the back door. "Arlene? Where's the Lava soap? Damn old truck engine was filthy." His hands were covered with black grease, and his sweaty face had two smudges. He was dressed in tattered overalls and no shirt. His surprise at seeing Robbie sitting there with his wife was unmistakable.

"Howdy, Robbie," J.T. said, recovering quickly. "Didn't know you were here." He had what Robbie always thought of as a beer belly, and it was the only thing that detracted from his overall appearance as an attractive man. He was in his late thirties, with blue eyes and blond hair. His classic lantern jaw and full lips were softened by a reddish blond moustache.

Robbie didn't know him well, and she'd never felt the urge to change that fact. "I brought some food," she said. "It was the least I could do."

Arlene had looked under the sink and silently handed J.T. the requested soap.

"Well, right kind of you, Robbie." J.T. turned on the faucet and began washing his hands and arms. He turned as he dried off. "Got an old engine out there in the barn I've been meaning to work on. Thought today might be a good time." He finished drying, nodded to Robbie, and headed to the front room of the house.

Robbie thought the idea of his working on a truck engine the day after his brother-in-law's death was a little odd; kind of disrespectful or something. She also idly wondered why he was working here at Eric's barn. He had a perfectly good garage over at his place. Maybe it was some

56

project he and Eric had begun.

Robbie asked about Winona's children, and Arlene said they were too young to realize exactly what was going on about their daddy.

"I'm thankful it was me that found him and not Chip or Tammy," Arlene said.

Robbie agreed that would have been a tragedy.

Arlene continued, "It's going to be powerful hard for me to forget finding Eric's body. I can still see him lying there on the garage floor. I'll dream about it for months. The only good thing is I won't have to carry around all that guilt like Winona."

"What guilt?"

"Winona knew Eric was sick, and yet she went off to her stupid writers' meeting anyway."

"Arlene, it's only natural. As I understand it, Eric wasn't that sick. Winona said she thought he had a stomach virus."

"If you ask me, she should have taken him to a doctor three days ago."

"Arlene, I knew Eric. Not well, I'll admit, but I did know him well enough to know that unless he was flat on his back there was no way anyone could get him to go to a doctor."

Arlene sniffed. "Maybe so, but all I can think about is if that heifer had taken my brother to the doctor, he would still be alive." Her voice dripped venom.

Robbie was shocked to her toes. Surely Arlene didn't mean what she was saying. She had to have known what a horse's patootie Eric was. "Arlene Saunders, I can't believe you're blaming Winona. You know Eric ruled this house. Winona couldn't even go to the toilet without his permission. If he decided he wasn't going to the doctor, then that was the end of it. She couldn't bodily drag him."

Arlene had the decency to blush. "Maybe you're right. I probably don't even know what I'm saying. I haven't slept since night before last."

"Oh, I'm sorry. I should go," Robbie said and stood. "You try and get some rest. Did the doctor give you a sedative?"

"Yes, but I don't like pills, so I didn't take any."

"Maybe you should this time."

They walked down the hallway to the side door and outside. Robbie remembered she had wanted to ask what Eric did. "Without sounding like a 'nosy-rosy,' are Winona and the kids going to be okay financially? I mean, did Eric have life insurance at work or something?"

"I'm sure I don't know," Arlene mumbled.

"I guess I've forgotten," said Robbie. "Who did he work for?"

"For himself." Arlene wouldn't look Robbie in the eye. She turned, stepped to the screen door and opened it, keeping her back to Robbie.

"Oh, I didn't realize," said Robbie. Arlene was acting uncomfortable about the questions, and she couldn't imagine why. It made her determined to find out what she could about Eric's work. "But he was still in sales, wasn't he?"

"Yeah, sales. Look, Robbie, I have to get back inside. They'll be wanting to eat soon."

"Oh, Arlene, I could stay and help if you want to rest." Robbie felt guilty because she hadn't offered to serve.

"No, no, that won't be necessary. There are enough aunts and in-laws to handle it. I'll just have to show them where things are." Arlene stepped inside the door and latched the hook on the screen with a snap.

Robbie could take a hint, but asked anyway, "Well, if you're sure?"

Arlene nodded.

"Tell Winona to call if she needs me. I can babysit the kids or whatever."

Arlene turned abruptly away from the door, and Robbie walked to her car, wondering why Arlene had suddenly gotten so upset. She opened the station wagon door and heard the screen door when it slammed behind her. She turned around, and J.T. was striding toward her.

"Robbie, darlin'," he said, "can we talk a minute?"

"Of course, J.T."

"Whew." He smiled and gestured toward the front yard. "Let's get out of this hot sun and into that shade."

Robbie closed her car door, and J.T. hooked his arm through hers as if they were best buddies and steered them over to a magnolia tree.

J.T. released her arm and turned to face her. "Robbie, I don't want you to get the wrong idea."

"Wrong idea about what?"

"Arlene's overwrought. That stuff she said about Winona and Eric. She was just mouthing off." J.T. had showered and shaved. His Western shirt was open at the neck and his aftershave had a woodsy scent. His blue eyes looked deeply into Robbie's brown ones as if she were the only woman in the world. "I never noticed before what beautiful eyes you have, Robbie."

Robbie was startled to realize J.T. was flirting with her.

Did he think she would be susceptible to his charm because she was an older woman? Some women might be, but not me, thought Robbie. Besides, being totally secure in her relationship with Damon made her impervious to his conceited charm. Anyone else, and she might have been a tiny bit flattered, but J.T. had some ulterior motive, and that made her curious. "I can understand about Arlene," she said, ignoring his remark about her eyes. "She's still in shock. I'm sure she doesn't realize what she

"That's right," said J.T. "Arlene looked u
brother. It was awful to find him like that. S
wants to blame someone. Winona just happ
the moment. Tomorrow it will be someon
even me." He flashed the big smile at her

"It's no big deal, J.T. I don't think badl

"Good, I feel better. Let me walk you bac
He lay his arm across her shoulder. "How
business? Damon staying busy?"

"Oh yes, he's busy, but he enjoys his w

J.T. opened the car door. "By the way
musta thought it was funny, me working or
gine while the rest of the family is in there
for Eric. Truth is, I have to go out of town
a job and get back for the funeral on Sun

Robbie lied through her teeth. "Pshaw
nothing of it." She climbed into the car an
gine. "You take care of Arlene and Win
They're going to need your strong should
When Robbie backed and turned her car, J
bye. She waved back and headed towards

IV

Robbie kept thinking about the encounte
did he think she needed an explanation a
what about that flirting? He was obviously
magnetism to try to distract her, but from
was up to something, and he didn't want

But as she kept thinking about him, u
wicked thought. Winona was an attractiv

nerable position in her unhappy marriage. Her husband gone much of the time. And when Eric was home, he was a brute. So along comes this sexy brother-in-law. Thinking about lovers' triangles and jealousies between Eric, Winona, Arlene, and J.T. occupied her mind as she straightened the house.

Robbie felt a headache coming on—the countryside was full of ragweed that caused her allergies to react. So when Mary Lou called to complain about Arlene and not getting to see Winona, she wasn't too sympathetic.

"It's nothing to do with you, Mary Lou," said Robbie. "I didn't get to see Winona either."

Mary Lou complained only a bit more before she changed the subject to her writing project. She'd just received a new reference book on poisons and planned to spend the entire evening reading it. Robbie's head pounded, and she was relieved when Mary Lou had to hang up and feed her cat.

Robbie took an antihistamine and a nap. By the time Damon came in, her headache was down to a minor dull ache.

"Did you talk to Winona today?" he wanted to know. "I drove out there before coming home, and Arlene said Winona was asleep."

"No, I was there this afternoon, but Arlene said Winona was sedated," said Robbie. "And Mary Lou called right after I got back. She was mad because she had gone out there around noon, and Arlene wouldn't let her see Winona."

"Isn't that odd? Her sleeping all day?"

"Well, some people get knocked on their cans from even one tranquilizer. I'm sure that's what happened to Winona. Sleep is probably the best thing for her right now."

"You look like you're not feeling too well yourself."

"Ragweed season."

"Why don't I get a pizza for dinner, and you won't have to cook. Pepperoni okay?"

"Sounds great. When you get back I'll tell you all about my encounter with a sexy young man today."

"I sure don't want to miss that." Damon took off for the pizza parlor.

Robbie was putting out paper plates when the telephone rang. This time it was Lilabeth complaining about Arlene and how she had not been able to see Winona.

"Arlene did the same with me and with Mary Lou," said Robbie. "She admitted she hasn't slept for two days. She doesn't know what she's doing or saying."

"All those relatives must be driving her nuts. I offered to stay, but she insisted I leave."

"And J.T. isn't any help."

"No way. In fact, when I was leaving, he came barreling out from the barn in this huge eighteen wheeler. Nearly ran over me."

"He was coming into town?"

"No, he turned off, heading north for Dallas," said Lilabeth. "Oh, I gotta hang up, Robbie, the baby's crying."

When Damon came back with the pizza, Robbie told him what Lilabeth had said about Winona and Arlene.

"Are you worried, hon?"

"Maybe. Just a little. I keep thinking Winona must be wondering why none of us has been around to see her."

"We could go out after we eat, but only if you feel up to it."

"I'm not sure we should. Maybe tomorrow."

"Well, I've got a few more questions for her, but they can wait until tomorrow," Damon said. "If she's been sedated all day, she won't be able to give coherent answers. You want to call?"

"I don't think so. I imagine their phone has been ringing off the wall, and I would just add to the confusion."

As they got ready for bed, she told Damon how J.T. had flirted with her and about her suspicions of him and Winona having an affair. "Maybe Arlene found out and told her brother," said Robbie. "Eric had such a volatile temper he would have confronted J.T."

"Sure, and Eric would have killed J.T. on the spot."

"What if they just had an argument then, and later on J.T. somehow got Eric to take the rat poison. Gave it to him in food or something to drink."

"Or maybe J.T. told Winona to get rid of Eric," said Damon, "so they could be together."

"Winona is my friend, and I just don't think she's capable of murder." Robbie crawled into bed.

"Anyone is capable of murder given enough provocation."

"I don't really believe that. I think some people would argue, fight, throw tantrums, do anything else, but never, ever commit murder."

"I can't see you ever killing someone."

"I could kill in an instant if anyone hurt you or one of our kids."

"I'm not so sure you could. Just how would you do it, anyway? Shoot them or poison them?" He got into bed beside her.

"I'd hack them up with an axe."

Damon was silent a moment before he laughed. "Okay, Miss Lizzie of Frontier City, you've made a believer out of me. Now we'd better get some sleep—tomorrow will be a busy day."

"Do we have to?"

"You have a better idea?"

She told him, and it was a while before they went to sleep.

V

Saturday was the only day Robbie and Damon Dunlap allowed themselves to lollygag, and they slept a good hour past their usual awakening time. Robbie hadn't slept well. She'd dreamt about Winona all night—bad dreams—but couldn't remember them. She told Damon she wanted to go see her friend.

Damon said, "If Arlene refuses to let me see Winona, I'll use my legal authority as sheriff to override her objections."

After breakfast they drove out in his county vehicle, a four-wheel-drive Ford Explorer. A cold front had moved down from the Panhandle overnight, and the day was crisp and hinted of autumn. High, wispy clouds raced southward toward the Gulf of Mexico. The Baldwin farm looked deserted when they arrived—no cars or sign of life.

"Looks like no one's here," said Damon as they got out and walked to the side door. He knocked, but got no answer.

"That's strange," said Robbie and walked to the front to peek into the windows. When no one responded to her knocking at that door, she walked to meet Damon, who had gone around to the back. "I guess everyone's in town at the funeral home or over at Arlene's."

"Could be. I'll call Dispatch and have them check at the funeral home."

Damon looked out at the barn, and Robbie looked too, shading her eyes with her hands.

"Damon, it looks like the barn's been remodeled. Why would they do that and let the house practically fall down?"

"I don't know." He stood there a moment thinking and then walked a couple of steps in the barn's direction before he stopped. "What was it you told me about J.T. working on an engine?"

Robbie had been getting ready to ask if he'd also send a deputy to Arlene's house, and it took her a second to comprehend his question. "Uh . . . He said he was working on this truck engine, getting ready to go out of town on business. He wanted to be back in time for the funeral tomorrow."

"And he was out in the barn? Not in the garage?"

"That funny yellow tape was still across the garage doors." Suddenly Robbie remembered something else. "Last night Lilabeth said J.T. came barreling out of here in a big eighteen wheeler. Almost ran her down."

"Hmmm," Damon said and began walking toward the barn.

"Damon?" He didn't stop. "Damon, where are you going? I think we ought to get back to town. I want to talk to Winona."

Damon ignored her. She started to follow, but he heard her and stopped long enough to say in a firm tone, "Wait for me in the car."

Robbie, torn between wanting to follow and wanting to do as he asked, stopped. She watched as he reached the barn and went inside. When he didn't come right back out, she slowly began walking toward the barn. Before she reached the door, Damon came out, grim-faced, carrying Winona Baldwin in his arms. Her small frame looked like that of a child in his big arms.

"Oh, my heavens," said Robbie. "Is she uh . . . ?"

"She's alive. Run! Call Dispatch! Tell them to send an ambulance." Damon walked steadily toward the house. "I think she's been drugged. I'm going to break in, try to revive her."

Robbie ran for the Explorer and the police radio.

Damon had just broken into the side door, picked Winona up again, and stepped inside, when Robbie came bursting in. "We'll have to take her. EMS had to respond to a car wreck over on I-35."

Robbie sat in back—holding Winona, talking to her, trying to wake her up. An emergency room team met them at the door with a hospital gurney, rushing Winona inside and out of sight.

An hour went by before a nurse came out and said they'd pumped Winona's stomach and they thought she'd be okay.

Damon told Robbie that he had to go back out to the Baldwin barn with a search warrant.

"What is going on, Damon?"

"Looks like this is all involved with those truck hijackings. That's all I can say."

VI

The cold front intensified, and the next evening Damon and Robbie were snuggled on the sofa in front of the fireplace. "Strange, isn't it?" Robbie mused as she sipped hot chocolate topped with marshmallows.

"How's that?"

"How you'd never have solved this case with your skewed ideas about poison. You thought it just had to be Winona who'd given Eric the arsenic. I was right about men being the chief poisoners historically. According to Mary Lou's poison book . . ."

"Okay, I've admitted I was wrong; don't rub my nose in it."

"Sorry." She snuggled closer to his side, pulling his arm tighter around her shoulder to let him know she was only teasing.

Damon started telling her what he'd found at the barn. "Eric and J.T. were hijacking trucks. The barn was full of stolen merchandise. Arlene says Eric got mad about something, maybe a fight over the profits. And Eric was going to talk to me—expose the whole operation."

"Was something going on between J.T. and Winona?"

"Arlene says not, but what else could she say? We'll probably never know for sure because J.T. isn't talking. Winona says she found out J.T. gave Eric the rat poison and she thinks he somehow got her to take the tranquilizers. Put them in her coffee probably. After the first ones," Damon said, "things got pretty hazy."

"Did Arlene know anything about the pills?"

"She's admitted she didn't try to stop it."

"What will happen to her?"

"She'll get immunity if she testifies."

Robbie pulled away from Damon's arm and sat upright.

"What's wrong, hon?"

"Nothing. I just thought of a great subplot for my book—how wife steers husband in the right direction to catch murderer. I want to write it down . . ."

Damon pulled her back down and gave her a kiss. "Okay, little helper, but not tonight. I've got a subplot of my own here we need to act out."

"Unh-huh," said Robbie. "In that case I'll write tomorrow, dear."

A One-Day Job

Even with deep creases around her mouth and eyes, and skin that was leathery—tanned by wind and sun—something about her presence told me Mrs. Gillingwater would be equally at home astride a horse or at a fancy dress ball. Her hair, pulled back in a long ponytail, was dish water blonde streaked with gray. "Ms. Gordon, I just don't know what to do or where to turn. Those people won't even talk to me, although I guess I can't blame them. They think Cord is responsible for Tyler's . . ." Her voice broke, but for only a moment; then she was back in control again. ". . . for their son's death." Worry was obvious in the line between her brows, and pain was even stronger in her pecan-colored eyes.

A woman obviously used to adversity, I had the feeling she could handle anything from a sick calf to a hailstorm destroying their cotton crop. She was descended from that breed of west Texas pioneer women I used to read about, the kind whose grandmothers fought smallpox and Indians and the stark landscape of early Texas.

Maudie Rae Gillingwater had come into G. & G. Investigations a few minutes earlier saying an Austin homicide lieutenant named Larry Hays had suggested she talk to us. He told her my partner and I might not be the best known private eyes in Austin, but we were good investigators.

Larry Hays had been my late husband's friend and partner for ten years before Tommy left the police department and opened an investigator's office. Larry had never been too generous with praise, but his attitude was

68

changing in recent months. And now he even referred clients to us sometimes.

"And you think, Mrs. Gillingwater, that these people know where your daughter is?" I asked.

"Please call me Maudie Rae," she said.

"Okay, Maudie Rae, and I'm Jenny."

"The Kents have to know where Megan is. She's been staying with them. But I'm also sure she told them Cord kicked her out and to keep us away from her." She was sitting on the edge of the chair as if she might leap up and walk out at any moment.

I wondered if she was uncomfortable talking to me, or if she just had trouble relaxing, period. I decided it was probably a little of both.

Suddenly, she blurted out, "All right, I'll admit I was the one who kicked her out, not Cord. But I didn't seriously mean it, and Megan knows that. She and I hadn't been getting along even before she got pregnant."

"How far along is she?"

"Almost six months." She shook her head. "Has it only been a month since we found out she was expecting? Seems like this thing has gone on forever."

I'd heard about the case, of course; it had been a hot topic for days. It began four weeks ago is Chisholm, Texas, when the Gillingwaters' daughter turned up pregnant. A few days after that her father had accosted young Kent in front of witnesses at the high school, threatening to kill the boy. And the two youngsters had run away—from the small west Texas town to Austin where the boy's parents lived.

The night they left, Gillingwater was again overheard threatening the boy. Two days after arriving in Austin, Tyler Kent had been shot and killed; yesterday Cordell Gillingwater had been arrested for the boy's murder.

The fact that Tyler Kent and Megan Gillingwater were sixteen years old had drawn a sympathetic press like stink on a hog-pen. Austin's news media had a feeding frenzy—the star-crossed lovers, a modern day Romeo and Juliet—hinted of tabloid-headline-type news. Reporters have always loved an underdog.

"How did Megan get involved with a boy from Austin?"

"Tyler was living with his grandmother in Chisholm. I don't know the details, but he and his father were in Chisholm taking care of some family business, and then the father left. The boy stayed and started to high school. He and Megan started dating during football season. Both parents came to Chisholm at Thanksgiving. Megan had dinner with them.

"That's when my daughter and I first had harsh words over Tyler. I thought she was too young to get serious over any one boy. She didn't want to hear what I thought."

How can mothers and daughters get so angry at each other and say such horrid things? (But what do I know about motherhood? I grew up without mine.) "And your daughter's only sixteen. That's underage, isn't it? Can't you force her to come back?"

"Legally, yes. I talked to your Lieutenant Hays about it," said Maudie Rae. "I learned I could go to court—get a writ of habeas corpus or some big legal term, and the Kents would have to show up in court with Megan. But all that legal stuff costs money, and I've already had to sell off a good-sized herd of cattle to hire a competent defense lawyer for Cordell."

"Who did you get?"

"Bulldog Porter."

"He's good, maybe even the best defense lawyer in the whole state," I said with a smile.

"I sure hope so for what he's costing."

"I'm surprised you were able to get him to take the case. He's been semi-retired for several months." Bulldog's seventy-eight years had finally begun to show after a case we'd helped him with a few months ago turned sour. The lawyer had had strong emotional ties to the young man involved, and C.J. and I had worried about Bulldog ever since—not knowing if he would ever snap back to his former self.

"Mr. Porter went to elementary and junior high school with my mother-in-law down in Galveston. They haven't seen each other for something like sixty years, but she asked for his help. He talked to Cord, and afterward said he'd defend him." She cleared her throat. "But he also wanted a ten thousand dollar cashier's check for deposit up front."

"That's probably standard."

"Even for the son of an old girlfriend? Looks to me like he'd be a little more trusting."

"One thing I know about Bulldog is that he always manages to get more serious about a case when someone is willing to put their money on the line."

"Maybe things are done like that in a big city, but out in Chisholm, Texas, a man's word counts for something."

"It is different in Austin, Maudie Rae. People get jaded and cynical in cities."

"Well, whatever. I did raise the money for Mr. Porter's fee, but it wouldn't be easy to scrape up another fee like that for another lawyer to get the Kents and Megan into court. I mean, we have the money, but Porter thinks he can get Cord's bond reduced. I'll need ten percent of however much that is to get him out of jail." She leaned back in the chair, rubbed her eyes and scratched the end of her nose with her thumb. "Oh, if worst comes to worst I can get cash from Mother Gillingwater, but Lordy, Lordy, that woman makes you pay two lifetimes of making up when she does a favor for you."

"I had a grandmother like that," I said. "Did you ask Mr. Porter if he could do the writ for you? Maybe for a reduced fee?"

"Yes, but he suggested I talk to you and Ms. Gunn first."

"And you've tried talking to the Kents yourself without . . ."

"I went over to the Kents' house, but Mr. Kent—I think his name is Gene—said he didn't know where Megan was and for me to get the hell off his property before he called the cops." She asked if I minded if she smoked, and when I said "no" she opened her purse and pulled out one of those thin cigarillos and lit it.

I opened a drawer and pushed an ashtray over to the edge of my desk for her as Maudie Rae continued talking.

"Mr. Kent was quite belligerent, cussing me out. I left because I was afraid he'd stroke out or I would. I've also called four times, but each time they hang up when they discover who's calling. If you'd be willing to find and talk to Megan, maybe you can talk some sense into that girl. The idea that she thinks her father would kill anyone is absolutely beyond belief."

"The police have charged him . . ."

"I know, but there's no way in hell that Cordell Gillingwater could have killed that boy, and Megan ought to be the first to admit it. He's the most tenderhearted man I've ever known. Everyone knows how he cries and leaves home just because it's time to cut the steers.

"Besides, we had just arrived in Austin the night Tyler was killed. Cord was exhausted. We had dinner in our rooms and went to sleep early."

"The police didn't believe you?"

"They said if I was asleep, how did I know Cord didn't leave the room?"

"And . . ."

"When you've been sleeping next to a man as long as I've been sleeping next to Cord—one thing is for certain—you might not wake up every time he goes to take a leak, but you sure as hell know when the bed is empty for more than five or ten minutes."

Her story had a ring of truth. Tommy and I had been married for ten years before he died, and although he was a cop and worked different shifts through the years, I'd always had trouble sleeping soundly in an empty bed. It was months after his death before I was able to sleep more than twenty or thirty minutes at a time.

My partner, an ex-policewoman named Cinnamon Jemima Gunn, better known as C.J., chose that moment to walk into the office. C.J. had been in Dallas conducting a seminar on tracing financial assets by computer. I introduced her to Mrs. Gillingwater and filled her in on what we were being asked to do.

Maudie Rae wanted to know what we'd charge to try to find Megan. Since C.J.'s the one who keeps our books, I usually defer those decisions to her.

"Two hundred a day plus expenses," said C.J. "It shouldn't take more than two or three days." She pulled out a contract from the file cabinet, handing it to Maudie Rae. "We'll need a deposit."

I watched Maudie Rae's face as she grimaced and spoke up. "Two hundred will be just fine, Mrs. Gillingwater." I ignored C.J.'s pointed stare.

Mrs. Gillingwater said she was staying at the Executive Suites Hotel as she gave C.J. the check. She signed the contract with a flourish, then opened her purse and gave us a photograph of her daughter. "When you find Megan, please tell her I love her. Tell her where I'm staying if she needs me."

As soon as the woman walked out the door, C.J.'s cola nut-colored face got that haughty Nefrititi look that I hate. She reminds me of that actress who played Lieutenant Uhuru on the original Star Trek, but when she puts on the Egyptian Queen's face—I'm in trouble. "Why did you butt in? You should always ask for a two-day minimum. When will you ever learn?"

My partner is six feet tall in her stocking feet, modeled in New York and Paris in her late teens before she became a cop. Normally she moves as gracefully as a panther, but when she's mad she stomps around like a linebacker. She stalked out to the front reception room to her desk and sat in her swivel chair.

I followed her and sat opposite. "I just felt sorry for her—the legal fees are eating her up already."

"Jenny, if what I've heard is true, those people have oil and cattle running out the yazoo. Not to mention cotton and . . ."

"And her pregnant sixteen-year-old daughter doesn't want to talk to her, and her husband is in jail for murder."

"Sheesh. Hard luck stories always make you act—"

"All you think about is money."

"Someone has to; you obviously never do."

"We've paid the rent this month. We've paid all the bills and taken out our salaries. What more do you want?"

"I'd like to be a little ahead instead of always scrambling. I'd like to be able to save . . ."

I started laughing. "Holy Cow. Would you listen to us? We sound like an old married couple."

C.J. could never keep a straight face when I get tickled. "You ain't never lied and you ain't even my type." Lapsing into the uneducated dialogue really set me off because C.J.'s a college graduate.

When I could talk again I said, "Okay. Look, two hundred is a one-day charge, and if the lady has assets like you say, she's good for the rest."

"Maybe. I'll know more when I run some computer checks on her." She turned on her computer and started her nimble fingers to work. "But next time when we get to the money part with a client, keep your mouth shut, bitch."

I walked into my inner office without saying anything, but when I reached the doorway, I turned and stuck my tongue out at her back.

"I saw that. Tacky, tacky."

"Bitches do things like that." How had she known?

She turned off the computer and opened the bottom drawer in her desk. "Get your purse and beeper, turn the answering machine on and let's go see if we can talk to Megan Gillingwater."

The Kents' house was on the edge of the Hyde Park area of central Austin. One of the oldest neighborhoods in the city, it still retained a genteel charm. The address we wanted was a house made of native rock, burnished a muddy brown by the weather, but freshly painted white shutters brightened it considerably. Oleanders bloomed at each corner and the flower beds which ran the length of the front were full of the bright colors of petunias, marigolds, zinnias, pansies and roses. Native pecan trees and one huge magnolia loaded with white full flowers gave the front yard shade, a welcome addition to the ninety degree weather of early May. A long driveway led to the back and a detached two-car garage.

I rang the doorbell which was quickly answered by a tiny woman about my age (thirty-five) with fuzzy blonde hair. She wore a white T-shirt emblazoned with Mickey Mouse and a pair of black denim shorts. She was barefoot. "Mrs. Kent?" I asked.

"Yes, yes. Come on in. I know I promised you an hour, but I really don't have that much time today." She turned and was halfway down the hall before I could answer.

C.J. and I looked at each other, shrugged and followed the woman who led us to a family room at the back of the house.

She gestured to the French doors which opened to a wide expanse of a St. Augustine lawn edged by crepe myrtle and mimosas, each in full bloom. Someone had spent many hours taking care of the outside. "We can go out back after you've seen the house."

"I beg your pardon?" said C.J.

"Mrs. Kent? I think there's been some mis . . ."

She looked at us expectantly and nodded towards the kitchen. "We might as well start in there. Are you taking photographs, too?"

". . . take. I don't think we're who you expected," I said.

"You mean you're not from Century Twenty-One?" she asked. "We're selling this house and . . ." She stopped. "Who are you, then?"

A slender teen-age girl whose abdomen pooched with pregnancy walked out of the kitchen and into the family room drinking a large glass of milk. It was Megan Gillingwater.

"Megan," I said. "I'm Jenny Gordon, and this is C.J. Gunn. We're private investigators. Your mother hired us to find—"

"Get them out of here," Megan said, but she didn't yell

or actually speak much louder than a stage whisper. "I don't want them anywhere near me." She paused, looking like a deer caught in the bright beams of an automobile, then ran across the room passing directly in front of me. I put out my arm to stop her, but she brushed it aside and headed into the hallway.

Mrs. Kent yelled, "How dare you come into my house!"

"Let's just everyone calm down and see if we can have a nice conversation here." I heard C.J.'s placating tone as I started after Megan, leaving C.J. to deal with Mrs. Kent.

I caught up with the girl when she reached a bedroom off to her right. She darted into the room, with me right behind and flung herself down on a big four-poster bed covered with a patchwork quilt.

"Megan, I only want to talk to you." The girl's shoulders shook with emotion. "Please don't cry. Listen a minute, and if you don't like what I'm saying, I promise I won't bother you anymore."

I thought she was going to ignore me, but finally she rolled over, sat up, showing me a profile. Her hair was long, almost to her waist, and looked like a honey-blonde waterfall cascading around her head. Her dark blue eyes were bright in her pale face.

She glanced at me, but let her eyes slide off mine and looked somewhere off to my left. She still didn't speak.

"Megan, your mother wanted me to tell you that your father did not kill Tyler. She says if you think about it rationally, you'll know she's telling the truth. That your father isn't capable of murder. She doesn't know who killed him, but please stop thinking it was your father."

"I don't want to hear any more. Please leave now." She turned her back to me in obvious dismissal.

"I'll go, but your mother wanted me to tell you if you

need anything or if you want to talk, she's staying at the Executive Suites Hotel."

Her voice was muffled at first when she said, "I will never, ever want anything from my mother." She still wouldn't look directly at me. "You tell her that, lady." Her voice was a monotone, and I strained to hear.

"And I never ever want to see her again either. Tell her to leave me alone," she said.

She tried, but failed to convince me that she meant it. That's when I saw the teardrop fall and watched as she brushed her cheek. I wanted to keep her talking. Something was going on here, but I didn't know what. "If that's what you want me to tell her, okay, but that's no way to treat the grandmother of your baby. Little kids need . . ."

The love-hate relationship with her mother took over, and she spoke up. "Don't throw that grandmother crap at me. She's not ready to be a grandmother yet. Said she was much too young."

"I'm sure she didn't mean it."

"Oh, she meant it. She made it perfectly clear. My mother never says something she doesn't mean." She got up from the bed and walked over to turn on a television. "Something else you should know about my mother. She leads my dad around by the balls. She tells him what to do, and he does it. He can't wipe his ass without her permission. If she told Daddy to do something about Tyler, my dad would probably do it."

"Do you think your mother would say something like that to your dad?"

"I guess so. I don't know," she whispered. Her flash of rebellion was obviously over.

Suddenly loud voices came from the family room where I'd left C.J. and Mrs. Kent. Gene Kent had come home in a bad mood, or maybe that's how he always was. "My wife asked you to leave, and Megan asked you to leave. I want you people out of this house right now, or I'm throwing you out."

C.J. wouldn't take threats like that from anyone. She was a black belt in TuKong martial arts and had a quick temper. And if he even tried to make her leave before she was ready, he might find himself on the floor looking up in stunned surprise.

I reached the room just in time to see what I'd been afraid of happening happen. I saw Kent grab C.J.'s shoulder as if to propel her out, and next he was on the floor writhing in pain before I could intervene. It was hard to tell with him lying prone, but he looked to be a fairly good-sized man. A brawny construction worker type. Size didn't matter to C.J.—she'd take on anyone if necessary.

Mrs. Kent stood in the doorway to the kitchen, hand over her mouth, but I thought I saw a brief flash of satisfaction on her face before a mask dropped down.

Megan, who had been close on my heels, hurried to Mrs. Kent. There was no mistaking the fear I saw in their eyes as they stood, arms around each other, looking down at the man of the house.

"C.J. Haven't I told you to ignore clods like that? Let's get out of here before things seriously escalate." I took one arm which she tried to shake off, but I got a vice grip and began steering her to the front door. "I'm sorry, Mrs. Kent. Please offer my apologies to your husband, too," I called back over my shoulder.

I managed to get C.J. inside my car. "Damn it, C.J., the man might file assault charges against you." I started the engine, and we drove away.

"No. Assholes like Kent wouldn't ever want to admit he

was bested by a woman." She was under control except for her voice.

"Something else happened before the shouting started." And I knew the answer before she told me. The signs had been there in both Megan and Mrs. Kent.

She was rubbing her arm where I had held on to drag her outside. "Kent came in," she said. "When his wife said who we were and what was going on, he knocked the tar out of her."

"But I didn't see any evidence . . ."

"You know the type; hits where it never shows. He got her in the stomach and alongside her head—around her ears—before coming after me."

"Then I'm glad you laid the bastard out." I headed the car to APD headquarters. We needed details on the Kent boy's case directly from Lieutenant Larry Hays.

We entered headquarters by the front door. There's a circular counter in the atrium lobby which looks more like a hotel or office building lobby. The cops all call it "the donut." Brick terrazzo covers the floor, and the walls are beige and burnt orange. After calling upstairs for Larry to escort us, the officer in the donut ignored us. I walked over to look at the old photographs of police cars and officers of Austin in the past.

After Larry greeted us, he led us to the third floor, where homicide occupies the south side. Things have changed since Tommy worked here. Most noticeable are the movable panels about five feet high which are covered appropriately in blood red carpet and divide desks into cubicles. It was a strange feeling to be in this department where my husband had often spent more hours in a day than he had with me.

We filled Larry in on what happened at the Kents, and

when I got to the part about C.J.'s demolition woman
moves, he stifled a cough that I felt sure was a disguised
laugh. "C.J., you're going to regret this in a day or two."

"It was worth it no matter what happens," she said.

"You know she seldom thinks before she acts," I said.
"Look, I know you don't have much time, but what can you
tell us about the case, and what evidence is there against
Cordell Gillingwater?"

"Since the case is still active, I can only tell you what's
already public knowledge. The murder weapon was found
under the front seat of his car. No fingerprints. He had a
strong motive, and he'd threatened the kid."

"And he doesn't have a strong alibi," I said.

"I'm much more interested in Mr. Kent," said C.J.
"Hell, I never even saw him before today, but I'll bet he's
got a rap sheet."

Larry nodded. "Several family disturbances, assaults,
drunk and disorderly. No convictions."

"Long history of violence. Could be something there between him and the son," I said.

"We looked at Kent closely, but there was nothing to
connect him to his son's death," said Larry.

"Well, I'd look again if I were you." C.J.'s voice was
harsh as she walked out, heading for the elevators.

"Tell her to keep that temper under control." Larry
smiled. "I'd hate to have to arrest her."

"I don't tell C.J. anything. I sometimes ask and sometimes plead, but . . ."

"I know, but remind her that just because she doesn't
like the asshole is no reason to arrest him for murder."

I caught up with C.J. at the elevator. "Let's go to the
Hyatt and have a couple of beers and a bunch of fajitas."

She smiled. "Sounds like my kind of evening."

★ ★ ★ ★ ★

The telephone woke me at six a.m. It was Lieutenant Hays, and his voice was grim. "Megan Gillingwater tried to kill herself. You want to meet me at Brackenridge Hospital?"

"I'll be there in thirty minutes." I hung up and called C.J.

"I knew something was going on with those people, but I haven't been able to figure all the ins and outs yet," she said. "Pick me up on your way?"

Larry Hays was sitting beside Maudie Rae Gillingwater in the ICU waiting room. "How is Megan?" I asked.

"They think she'll be okay," said Larry. "She took some pills."

"The biggest worry is for the baby," said Maudie Rae. Our client's face showed she'd been crying, but was holding up pretty well. "I'm waiting to go in to see her." I gave her a hug, and tears filled her eyes, briefly. Then a nurse came and said she could go see her daughter.

C.J. went to find some coffee, and Larry and I walked out into the corridor. Several people were in the waiting room, and we wanted to be able to talk without bothering them.

"Where's Mrs. Kent?"

"Home, I guess. I think she's the one who called 911, but I'm not sure."

"This is her dead son's girlfriend here. The baby is her grandchild, too. You'd think she'd want to be here."

"Nothing about any of these people seems right to me," he said.

"You mean the Kents?"

"I mean both the Kents and the Gillingwaters."

"Maudie Rae seems like a pretty good old gal. I haven't met Cordell."

"He's about like you'd imagine a west Texas rancher to be—strong and silent. But I think she's capable of most anything."

"Ms. Gordon?" It was Maudie Rae. "Megan wants to see you."

Larry started to follow too, but the nurse in the pale pink scrub suit who was waiting to escort me to Megan's bedside said, "She said only Ms. Gordon."

The private room Megan Gillingwater had was small, and there was a window with a desk-type ledge and a pass-through box on one side of the door. The nurses could stand outside to do their paperwork and keep an eye on the patient at the same time.

The girl was pale against the bed sheets and looked about twelve. Her blonde hair was matted, and there were plastic tubes leading to veins and one to her bladder. Wires ran to machines and a blood pressure cuff was wrapped around her right arm. I could see a green pulsing light on one monitor, and another one had red numbers that kept flashing. The blipping noises sounded loud. That's when I realized it was monitoring the baby's heart and pulse rate.

Her eyes were closed, but she opened them when the nurse told her she had company.

"Hello, Megan."

She licked her lips and stammered a little. "Uh, sorry. I wanted to, uh, talk to you."

"Okay, Megan. You're doing just fine."

The nurse said I could stay five minutes and pushed a chair over for me before leaving. She could see us through the plexiglass window and watch the machines which also monitored Megan's heart rate and blood pressure.

Megan spoke hesitantly and the words came out in

broken sentences. "I couldn't get away from him, uh, I tried, but he hit mc again and again. In the stomach."

"Mr. Kent?"

She nodded. "The only way to get help was to take the pills. He said he would kill me, my baby and his wife too, if I told anyone or left the house." She gulped. "Gene Kent raped me," she said. "The baby's not Tyler's, but Tyler found out." Tears ran down her cheeks and splashed on the hospital gown.

It was something out of a nightmare. Poor kid! She'd been raped, assaulted and intimidated.

"My father didn't kill Tyler either," she said. "But I saw him die. His father did it."

"Mr. Kent killed his own son?"

She nodded, and great heaving sobs began which set off an alarm on the machines. The nurse came in and talked soothingly to Megan.

"I didn't do anything," I told the nurse.

"I know. She agitated herself." She smoothed back Megan's hair and said, "Take slow, long breaths. Think about lying back on fluffy white clouds and floating in a warm summer breeze. Breathe, breathe."

The heartbeat sounds slowed, and the nurse told Megan to keep taking the rhythmic breaths. "Maybe you should talk to Mrs. Gordon a little later, Megan."

"No. Have to tell, uh, before something else happens. I didn't want to come down here, but Tyler insisted we confront his father about the rape. That's when Gene Kent killed Tyler. Then he wouldn't let me leave the house or talk to anyone. And I'm still scared because . . ."

"Mrs. Kent's in danger?"

She nodded and closed her eyes.

"Okay, honey," I said. "I'll take care of it." I stood, but

she opened her eyes, and her look of despair was almost tangible.

Suddenly she began twisting and turning. "Owww, it hurts. My belly hurts. He hurt my baby." The alarm on the monitor went off again. Another nurse rushed in and said I'd have to leave.

I overheard one nurse, I didn't know which, say in a stage whisper, "She's getting ready to abort."

I backed out of the room. What should I tell Maudie Rae? That Megan had cleared Cordell? And what about the baby? I certainly didn't feel qualified to say that Megan might lose the baby.

For the time being, I decided the less said the better. When I got back to the waiting room I told Maudie Rae that Megan was fine, but that I needed to talk to Lieutenant Hays alone for a few moments. I could tell she wanted more details, but she'd wait if necessary.

Larry and C.J. knew me well enough to know what I had to say was important and followed me into the hallway without asking any questions. C.J. handed me a Styrofoam cup with coffee as we moved far enough away to keep from being overheard.

I told them what Megan had said, and C.J. said, "I just had a feeling that scum-bag was bad news."

Larry said, "I'd better send a patrol car over to check on Mrs. Kent." He said he'd fill us in later and took off.

When we got back to the ICU waiting room, a nurse was talking to Maudie Rae. When I heard the news that Megan had lost the baby, I couldn't help feeling some relief for the girl. Things will be much better this way, I thought.

Later that evening, as C.J. and I sat outside on my patio, Larry Hays telephoned to say Mrs. Kent had disappeared, but Gene Kent had been arrested.

"Do you think he killed her?" I asked.

"I think it's highly probable. I think when Megan went to the hospital Kent knew it was all unraveling and maybe the wife said something about going to the police. We may never find out what happened, and we may never find her unless Kent decides to confess."

"Ask Larry about Gillingwater," C.J. said.

"I heard her," he said. "We've released him, and I imagine he's at the hospital with his family."

I hung up the receiver and turned to C.J. "We cleared this up in one day. Now, aren't you glad I didn't get any more than two hundred dollars from Maudie Rae? I know how you hate to refund money."

"Lucked into it this time, didn't you? But next time . . ."

"I'll keep my mouth shut when it's time to discuss money."

I leaned back in my lounge chair, feeling pretty satisfied with myself, took another sip of my beer and watched some thunder heads roll in from west Texas.

Kiss or Kill

"Either Zachary went temporarily berserk and killed them," said C.J., "or Ola Mae Jordan did it."

"Your client?" I asked. We were sitting in the offices of G. & G. Investigations, jointly owned and operated by C.J. Gunn and myself, Jenny Gordon.

"She's not my client anymore," said C.J. "I told her two days ago I couldn't keep taking her money because it looked to me as if a judge and jury would have to decide her son's guilt."

"And?"

"She was furious. She ranted for ten minutes about me sending innocent blood to prison." C.J. jumped up and began pacing the floor. She stopped in front of me, her voice as raucous as a fishwife. "Said I'd been hanging with Whitey too long. Called me an 'Uppity Bitch' who's forgotten her place, and then she stormed out of the office."

My WASP parents brought me up to accept people as they are, not by what color they happen to be. And I despise prejudice in any form, but because I am white, I don't always notice racial slurs made, especially from one black to another. Yet even I caught these by Ola Mae Jordan.

C.J. sometimes has a short fuse, and I wondered if her reaction had been as swift and volatile as it had been to that dumb patrolman the night of her cousin Veronica's murder. The patrolman had made a sexist and racial remark and the next thing he knew, he was on the floor holding his manhood and throwing up his guts.

"Cinnamon, am I to understand you let her leave under

87

her own power after saying something like that?"

"Yassum, Miz Gordon. Sum times ya jest haveta con-si-der the source. Sum folk jest too iggnert to botha wid."

When Cinnamon Jemima Gunn started talking her southern black dialect, I usually cracked up. The vernacular is always funny coming from a Rice University alumni, a woman whose looks and elocution earned her top dollars in New York and Europe as an actress/model in her younger days. Today, I barely managed a smile. Being on target about Ola Mae was too true for it to be very humorous.

Another reason I had trouble smiling was because of something I saw in C.J.'s dark eyes. A strange blackness which didn't have anything to do with eye color and which had not been evident in her eyes fourteen days ago when I left for Phoenix for a visit with Tommy's parents. I could also tell her attempt at humor was forced. "Has it been that bad?"

C.J.'s eyes clouded. Although she tried to smile, her lips were tight and thin. "Worse, much worse."

For about eighteen months now, C.J. and I have slowly established a friendship. It began when we found the people who killed Melody Gunn, her eighteen-year-old baby sister, and my husband, Tommy Gordon. One thing I'd quickly learned was not to question her too closely when she got that haughty Nefertiti look.

She nodded again emphatically without speaking.

I got up and went into our lounge/store room to make coffee. The death of C.J.'s young female cousin and her cousin's baby had obviously been a nightmare. Maybe Veronica's murder had brought up all the grief of losing her little sister, but I had a feeling it was some deeper hurt.

When the coffee was ready I filled two mugs and walked back into the front office. I handed C.J. a cup and walked over to look outside at the dreary gray day in central Texas. On a normal day if you looked out our fourth floor window in the LaGrange Building, the Mo-Pac Freeway was visible. Today, a light fog swirled and shrouded the highway, and cars driving the north/south thoroughfare would appear and disappear in the mists. Their headlights bounced off the moisture and gave things a weird glow. It was almost what I'd imagined a misty landscape of Venus might look like with space vehicles roaming the area.

Probably fifteen or twenty minutes had gone by during which neither of us spoke a word, but I knew when I settled myself in the overstuffed customer chair in front of her desk that she had made a decision to tell me what was bothering her. Her eyes brimmed with tears, but none fell.

"Going into Veronica's house that night and seeing her . . ." C.J.'s voice held a tremor. "Seeing the blood spattered everywhere. And knowing little Zack lay dead in his crib . . . brought up things I didn't want to remember. Things I've tried to forget for five years."

One technique I'd learned from C.J. in the months we've worked together was when someone starts spilling their story, keep your mouth shut. Don't stop the flow of words.

"I lost a baby daughter," she said. "My husband and my baby. You know I worked for Pittsburgh PD back then."

I nodded.

"For months I'd worked on one case and finally got enough evidence to take down some heavy-duty guys. A couple of politicos. In bed with a cocaine syndicate. We made the arrests, and I was up for a promotion.

"A short time later, on a Sunday morning, my husband dressed our little one-year-old daughter. They were going to buy doughnuts. My car was in back of his in the driveway. I was still half asleep when the bomb went off.

The force of the explosion tore a hole into my kitchen wall and knocked me out of bed."

Listening to her recitation of the facts you would have thought she was talking about someone else—not her own family. But the pain etched on her face was unmistakable. "No more, C.J.," I said. "That's enough." I wanted desperately to offer some sympathetic word, yet instinctively knew it wouldn't be adequate. What I blurted out was, "Just tell me you got the slimy bastards."

She didn't answer. She didn't have to because the look in her eyes showed too much satisfaction.

"All right then," I said. "Let's put our heads together and concentrate on taking care of this slime-ball."

When she'd regained her composure she said, "The only people left to suspect are Veronica's ex-husband, Zachary Jordan or his mother, Ola Mae Jordan, who is my aunt.

"Now, I know my aunt didn't do it. She's too old and doesn't have the stomach to kill a cockroach. Zachary is still a possible. He was the one found over the baby's crib with a butcher knife in his hand, but every fiber in me says he didn't do it.

"I have trouble believing my aunt could kill anyone. I doubt she'd have the stomach for it. Especially with a knife. Which left Zachary as the major possible. He was the one found over the baby's crib, with a butcher knife in his hands, but then I have a hard time seeing him do it.

"He was off drugs, working and trying for a reconciliation with Veronica. Sure, he could have flown into a rage because Veronica wanted no part of him anymore, and offed her, but kill his little son? I don't think so."

"Doesn't sound likely, does it?" I agreed. "A random killing? An interrupted burglary?" C.J. shook her head. "So let's go back to the mother," I said. "Your ex-client. What's her motive?"

"Well, I know she hated Veronica. Blamed her for all the misery in their marriage. Even said Veronica was the one responsible for getting Zachary on drugs. Not true. He did that all on his own."

"I've heard all the old-battle-ax jokes about mothers-in-law and they're not funny. But let's say Ola Mae did hate Veronica enough to kill her. But how could she kill that baby; her only grandchild? And use a knife?"

"Well, it had me stumped, but once I tried thinking out of the box, the solution became simple. I've had doubts that Ola Mae could personally kill anyone, but a large sum of money can always hire a killer," said C.J. "With this in mind, I checked a little deeper into her boyfriend's background."

"Oh, ho. The mother has a boyfriend?"

"A dude named Luther Dawson. A dude fifteen years younger than Ola Mae with no visible means of support. A man who drives a brand new Cadillac and spends money so freely that everyone remembers him wherever he goes."

C.J. got up from the desk and she, too, looked out the window.

We P.I. types keep hoping inspiration will be written in the sky or something, I guess. "What else did you find out about old Luther?" I asked.

"He's got a history of violence—a long record—including assault and prison time for using a knife. He does like expensive things and does whatever he can to get the money to indulge himself. He's a braggart, too. Likes to play to an audience when he's flashing money."

"Sounds better all the time."

"I also found out from gossip, hearsay and the assorted unnamed sources that while it's true Ola Mae didn't want

Zachary and Veronica to get back together, she absolutely did not want Veronica to marry anyone else. Especially not the jazz musician Veronica had been dating for a few months."

"But why?" I asked, and then the light dawned. "Ola Mae was afraid if Veronica remarried she and her new husband would move away. That would make it nearly impossible for Ms. Jordan to see her grandbaby as often as she wanted. A musician would be someone who probably moved around a lot." I began to doodle on a note pad lying on the desk.

"Okay," I said. "Let's say this Luther Dawson was hired to get rid of Veronica. Veronica fought him like a wildcat. From what you said, the crime scene indicated that. And after he killed your cousin, something happened. We don't know what or how or why, but he killed the baby, too.

"Luther leaves and along comes the ex-husband father, Zachary, and he goes into the house for some reason and finds Veronica. His first thought is now for his son's safety. He runs to the nursery, and the baby is dead. He can't believe his son is dead. The knife is right there in the crib. He picks it up and . . . in walks the police."

C.J. walked back to the desk and watched me doodling. "It's the only explanation that makes any sense to me. I can't believe Zachary or Ola Mae could kill little Zack. And I know Ola Mae was upset over that grandchild's death. I also know she had this weird thing, an obsession for her son. It's not healthy, whatever it is."

"Okay. So do we work on Ola Mae? See if she will implicate Luther in some way?"

C.J. shook her head. "I think we'd be better off working on Luther. Ola Mae's never going to admit to any part of this. That bitch is too stubborn. And I think Luther is already tired of Ola Mae. He's been seen with a couple different younger chicks. Maybe he's ready to make a break."

She'd already given it some thought. "You have an ace up your sleeve?"

Her teeth flashed brilliant against her cola-nut skin as she smiled. "When you're hot, Baby, you're hot. Remember a couple years ago how an attractive undercover female agent dated a suspect who liked to talk so much, that he soon told her the whole story?"

"I remember. That was for one of those big name detective agencies, wasn't it?"

She nodded. "I've already made my move on Luther, using my natural charms and all. I met him night before last, but put him off when he asked me out. Told him I might be free soon. I think a little nudge in the right direction, and Luther will be eating out of my hand. He'll want to impress me, and he just might say something incriminating."

"You're something else, C.J. Old Luther ain't going to know what hit him. But the best part is I get to hide and watch sweet Cinnamon in action."

"And I'll be wired so you won't miss a single word."

That afternoon, C.J. and I spent time at a firing range. My late husband had been a police officer for a number of years, and he'd taught me to shoot. When C.J. and I formed our agency she had insisted we both keep in practice weekly. In Texas, only law enforcement officers are legally permitted to carry guns, but many investigators lived by the old adage—"I'd rather be judged by twelve than carried off by six." When the occasion called for it C.J. and I were prepared.

Dealing with Luther Dawson, who had a penchant for violence, meant one of us should go armed. I was it. My

Smith and Wesson would accompany me as I hung around listening to C.J. and Luther.

Through trial and error we determined the best place for her wire was taped to the center of her back. We didn't consult our friend, Lieutenant Hays. No one could claim entrapment if no one knew about it beforehand.

Two evenings of listening to C.J. and Luther was an education. It was the only thing that kept me from getting bored. She was having fun while I sat nearby monitoring everything.

On the third night, they'd been out to dinner and decided to make it an early night. The implication was that C.J. could be talked into spending the night with him. They were driving C.J.'s LeBaron convertible, and as they were listening to reggae music when they pulled in front of his place, they stayed in the car.

Suddenly, I heard C.J. talking, and she was going for it.

C.J.: "Luther, honey. I don't know why you don't just tell the old bag you gotta split. Tell her you're a big boy, and you need to move on." There was a brief silence and Luther groaned.

C.J.: "Ummmmm. A fine big fella you are."

LUTHER: "You don't understand, Baby. I can't do it."

C.J.: "I want us to have some fun. I'm tired of this winter damp, and I want to go someplace and toast in the sun. Maybe down to Mexico or Jamaica way. Just the two of us. The beach, the sun, the margaritas. And I'm ready to leave now. My bags are packed."

LUTHER: "I can't. Not yet. But I promise you it won't be long. A week. Hold off for a week, and I'll go with you."

C.J.: "What's the big deal? You tied to her umbilical?"

LUTHER: "It's not like that. It, uh, it's just Ola Mae

owes me some money. Lots of money. And she won't have it till next week. I don't like to go off and not have no greenbacks."

C.J.: "Like how many greenbacks we talking 'bout?"

There were some kissing noises and some unintelligible sounds, and Luther groaned again.

C.J.: "How much money, Luther?"

LUTHER: "Fifty thousand."

C.J.: "Sheeitt. What'd you do? Kill somebody?"

LUTHER: "Yeah."

C.J.: "Yeah? Well, hell. You mean you really wasted somebody for her? Who?"

I was sweating by then, afraid she was blowing it. It was too soon. But Luther didn't seem perturbed.

LUTHER: "No more, beautiful. I can't say . . . If I don't get a few things straightened out with Ola Mae, she could send me to Huntsville for the next hundred years. Or I might even wind up in that little room taking that lethal injection. So there's no way I can leave right now."

Bingo. We had it, we had enough. I picked up my car telephone and called Lieutenant Larry Hays at home. He said he'd be right over.

As I hung up, I saw Luther and C.J. strolling up to the front door and into the house. I felt some apprehension about her going inside with him, but I wasn't really worried. At least, not until a couple of minutes later when I heard a strangled sound.

LUTHER: "What's this. You got a wire on? You bitch. A frigging wire."

The last I heard before the microphone crunched was C.J.'s scream.

Damn. Larry hadn't arrived yet, but I couldn't wait. Everything had turned to shit. Grabbing my .38 police special out of the glove compartment, I raced to the front door. It was locked.

I looked through the front window, but the living room was dark. I finally made out a sliver of light coming from behind a closed door, down a hallway.

I kicked at the front door. It was solid and didn't budge. I kicked again in frustration, but knew I didn't have enough strength. I strained my ears, trying to hear what was going on, hoping Luther didn't have a gun. All I heard was my own pleading, "Please, please, don't let him kill her."

I had to get inside. I turned, jumped off the front porch and fell to the ground on one knee. I pushed upright and ran around the house to the back. A faint glow from the street light which was catty-corner from the house helped.

At the back corner, I paused. It was darker here—full of shadows. I heard a door open. Then a deeper shadow detached itself and moved towards me. It was the darker bulk of a stocky man. "Freeze," I said, pointing the S & W at him.

He kept coming, moving fast before I could react. He hit my right arm just as I fired, sending a sharp current of pain all the way to my neck.

The noise of the gun was deafening and blinding. I screamed and felt the gun leave my hand, falling free.

The man's fingers were suddenly against my throat. It was Luther. His weight knocked us both to the ground. The fall jarred me silly for a brief moment.

My right arm felt numb, but I kicked out and managed to connect the foot somewhere on his body.

Luther groaned and yelled. "Be still, Bitch. I've got you now." He caught my right foot and held it.

He was crazy if he thought I was going to just lie there. My vision was clearing, but blurry. The grass was damp and cold, and I rolled to my left side, still kicking out at him, but not connecting solidly enough to do any damage. If I could have seen better, it would have helped.

I managed to get free for a second before his big hand got a better grip on my right ankle.

He began dragging me towards him, and I could smell his sweat and my fear. His fingers were so tight they pinched my skin as he grabbed my free ankle and held on, but I ignored the burning pain and kept trying to pull free. "The cops are on the way, Luther. You'd better run like hell while you have a chance."

He kept trying to put both my ankles into one hand, and I was trying to kick loose. My hands were free, and I fumbled around in the grass. If I could only find a rock or a tree limb, I thought. I could hit him, maybe knock him back off me.

My left hand could reach farther, and I did find what felt like a lead pipe. I grabbed it. It was my gun. My right hand still felt funny, the fingers tingly, but I managed to hold the gun and got the hammer pulled back. The click sounded loud in the quiet air.

"Turn me loose, you scum-bag. Or so help me, I'll blow you sky high."

Inexplicably, I heard the back door slam, and then suddenly we were spotlighted by bright lights coming from somewhere. Neither Luther nor I moved. It was as if I'd just invoked the X-ray technicians' favorite phrase: "Don't breathe, don't move."

The lights weren't in my face, but shone directly on Luther's. I could see terror in his face.

Quicker than anyone could think about it, C.J. was standing above me, swinging something at Luther. It was a heavy iron skillet.

The skillet struck Luther's head, he fell over and C.J. looked down at me. "I couldn't let you shoot him, Girl-friend. We need him to testify against Ola Mae."

I was weak, giddy with relief. I couldn't help the chuckles that began bubbling up from inside me and erupted. C.J. caught it from me, and when Larry Hays and two patrolmen walked up, they ragged us for awhile about the skillet. Soon they were laughing with us as they handcuffed Luther.

C.J. related how she'd struggled with Luther when he found the wire and how she'd been knocked down. She'd hit her head and been dazed for a few minutes. When she staggered out to the kitchen and looked out the back door, she saw Luther and me and picked up the nearest weapon: the iron skillet.

She had a small goose egg and a cut on her head. "Nothing an ice pack won't cure," I told her.

The police had called the emergency medical crew who decided maybe Luther needed to go to the hospital for emergency treatment. He was awake, but a little incoherent. We followed along, so C.J. and I could be checked over, too.

Once at the hospital, it didn't take long for Luther to regain full consciousness. Larry read him the Miranda rights, and Luther started talking. He wasn't about to take a fall all by himself.

He cried when he told of killing the baby. That had not been part of the plan. The struggle with Veronica had taken much longer, and as she fought with him, little Zack awakened. The child began crying and screaming. By then, Luther's nerves were out on edge. He tried to calm the child, but little Zack only wanted his mother. Luther said he didn't know what happened, but somehow the baby stopped crying, and when he looked down, the baby was dead.

"Good police work, ladies," said Larry as the three of us walked out of the hospital.

"It will be when you pick up Mrs. Jordan," I said. I was calmed enough to feel almost normal, except for a slight tingling in my fingertips.

C.J. had been pronounced well enough to go home. She spoke up and squelched any doubts I might have had about the state of her health. "That's one bust I'd like to witness, Lieutenant."

"The warrant just came through. Let's go pick her up," Larry said and held his car door open for C.J. and me.

The Man in the Red-Flannel Suit

Christmas was supposed to be a candy-making, turkey-baking time, I thought. With furtive trips to buy gifts to hide, special gifts for someone special. A time of joy and laughter, and singing carols about peace on earth and about the spirit of love.

"Merry Christmas, Zoe," someone called out as I walked out the back door of HPD headquarters. I didn't recognize the voice.

"Merry Christmas," I said, but under my breath muttered, "Bah, humbug." Christmas was meaningless when your husband was in a coma in a nursing home with no hope of recovery, but there was no sense reminding people about Byron Barrow. Don't think I feel sorry for myself. Sure, I did for awhile, but you have to go on. Put the past out of your mind and keep on trucking. It's just that I'd rather forget about Christmas if no one minds.

It was sixty degrees in Austin, Texas, on the evening of December twenty-second, and my ROP unit (Repeat Offenders Program), along with the other members of a special drug task force, had busted a crack house at midnight.

I had volunteered to work all week including the twenty-fourth and twenty-fifth to allow some of my fellow officers to be off with their families for Christmas. It was pointless to let myself think about Christmas two years ago, the last one Byron and I had shared before he was shot in the head and left in his present condition.

My unit was part of the back-up team, and we'd hung back, letting the other team members take care of their jobs.

100

We arrested three suspects, but the house had been full of people. Four little children belonging to two of the suspects ran around crying, begging us not to take their mama and daddy to jail.

The other people in the house weren't related to the children or didn't want to be responsible for four kids, and we'd had to call Child Services. It was a heartbreaker right here at Christmas time.

After the bust my unit returned to headquarters to take care of the paperwork. Everyone was still pumped—adrenaline highs—it always happens. You get up for the operation, and when the bust goes well you can stay up for hours.

"Hey, Zoe. Did you see that Dude trying to get out the window? I was standing on the ground right beneath it, and he nearly climbed out on top of me," said Corky. "Man, he was so surprised he almost wet his pants."

"Yeah, Corky. I saw." Corky was from narcotics, and I'd known him for years. He's normally a quiet guy until after a big bust, and then he'll talk your leg off.

"Zoe, check out this card," said Brad, one of the DEAD agents. The card was a depiction of Santa and his sleigh sitting on top of an outhouse, with Santa yelling curses at Rudolph and the other reindeer. Brad opened the card and read the inside message aloud, "I SAID THE SCHMIDT HOUSE, YOU FOOLS!"

I'd probably seen the card six times already, but I laughed anyway.

It was after two in the morning when I finished my part of the necessary paperwork. Some of the team was going for breakfast at Denny's, but I begged off, saying I was tired and needed my beauty sleep. They pushed a little, but I reminded everyone I was due back on duty at ten a.m., and they gave up and left.

My adrenaline had already ebbed and, although I wasn't quite as tired as I'd made myself out to be, I was ready to get home.

I entered the parking garage of the old patrol building. It felt good to climb into the '92 Mustang I was driving this month. The ROP unit confiscates vehicles, and we used them as undercover cars.

This time of year the ground can still be warm, and when the air cools fog forms, especially in the low-lying areas. A few tendrils of fog clutched at my car, and I had to use the wipers to clear the wetness from the windshield. Fortunately the drive south on I-35 was short—exit on East Riverside Drive, cross the bridge, and head west.

The Texas Colorado River which meanders across central Texas has been dammed in numerous places, forming a chain of lakes. One of the smaller lakes known as Town Lake sits in the midst of downtown Austin. The major portion of the downtown area is on the north shore of the lake and my apartment complex is on the south shore a few blocks west of the Interstate.

Riverside Drive makes multiple curves following the lake's contours. With no traffic to speak of at that hour and because I knew the area like the inside of my mouth, I was driving at a good rate of speed. The moisture and fog in the air made it necessary to keep the headlight beams on low; otherwise I never would have seen the bundle of clothes in the right hand lane.

I thought I saw the clothes bundle move. My foot tapped the brakes automatically, and I came to a complete halt a few feet past the bundle, then backed slowly until it was in front of my right fender. I backed up a little more and steered my car into the same lane as the clothes, my headlights bathing the scene in a surreal light.

"Oh shit. Tell me I'm not seeing this," I said, but there was no mistaking the fact the clothing bundle was a woman lying in an awkward position on the pavement. A small girl was hunkered down almost on top of the woman.

I got out and walked over. The little girl looked to be about three or four years old, her long hair curling slightly in the dampness. The woman's neck was in an unnatural position, and I knew without even checking that she was dead.

The child was patting the woman's face, blood and all, saying over and over, "Mommy, wake up. Get up, Mommy."

I did a quick visual check of the child, who didn't seem to have any noticeable injuries. The woman had cuts and abrasions on her face, nothing that looked terribly bad.

There wasn't any doubt in my mind about what had happened. A car had hit the woman, flinging her into the air, and her neck had snapped when she fell.

I walked back to the Mustang, switched on the walkie-talkie and reported the accident to Dispatch. I took off my windbreaker and went back to the child. I wrapped it around her unprotesting shoulders and began talking to her. "Honey, I've called for some help for you and your mommy. Why don't you come with me to the car?"

The child kept begging her mother to get up. I don't think she even heard me.

I kept talking quietly to her, hoping to keep her from panicking. She became less agitated, but didn't answer. The calls to her mother eventually stopped. Moments later, a squad car and EMS wagon pulled up and the medical attendants took over, one picking up the child to examine while the other began his futile attempt to revive the woman. There was nothing they could do, but by law they had to try.

I told them I was Zoe Barrow, showed my ID, and said I had no idea when the accident had happened. "It probably couldn't have been more than ten, fifteen minutes. Otherwise someone else would have found her. Called it in."

"Even if someone saw them, they might not want to get involved," said the EMS guy who was holding the child.

"Well, it's not too easy to see along here, but how could anyone leave a child?"

"Go figure," he said.

There was nothing to identify the woman on her person, and from the looks of her and the daughter, they were probably homeless. Once the medical guy had completed his examination of the girl, I carried her to my car and put her inside. She didn't protest; she just looked back over where her mother was, soundless.

"My name's Zoe. What's your name, honey?"

"April."

"That's a pretty name." She looked at me, her big brown eyes like a fawn's. "How old are you April? Do you know how old you are?"

She held up four fingers and said "four" softly.

"Four. You're a big girl, aren't you? What's your mommy's name?"

She looked puzzled and finally said, "Mommy."

"Okay. Do you know where you live?"

April shook her head.

"Where's your daddy?"

She didn't answer. She tucked her head down to her chest and began crying, but in a moment she stopped and looked at me and said, "Santa Claus."

Oh, Lord. For a minute I'd forgotten it was Christmas. "Well, yes. Santa Claus will come to see you soon." And vowed that I would make sure Santa brought April a toy or two.

But as I spoke, April began sobbing again. This time it was worse—not exactly heartrending. This time I thought I heard fear in her voice. I put my arm around her and tried to hold her, but she pulled back. Was she afraid of me?

Better to let her cry it out a bit, I thought. Maybe she'd tire and go to sleep. Probably be the best thing for her.

Accident investigators (we call them A.I.s), a police photographer, patrol officers and the medical examiner had all arrived while I was talking to April. I saw several patrol officers making a methodical search of the area, poking in the grassy weeds along the shoulder of the street. I knew they were hoping to find clues about the accident or something that would identify April's mother.

The A.I. in charge came over. I got out of my car and gave him an account of what I'd seen. Which didn't take long. He asked me to stop by headquarters later and make a formal statement. I assured him I would and started to get back into the car.

One of the patrol officers came over and handed me a teddy bear. "We carry these in the trunk of our units to give to kids. It usually helps if they have a pal."

"Great idea. Thanks."

I got back into the car, and April grabbed the bear I held out as if she were drowning and I'd just thrown her a lifeline. Tears still glistened on her face and in a few minutes she started making that funny sub-sub noise kids make when they've cried a lot. I patted her shoulder, and she leaned her head back hugging the bear tightly. Her eyelids were getting heavy. I didn't try to talk to her or hold her. As long as she was quiet, it was probably best to leave her alone.

The mother's body was covered with a blanket. Measurements were taken of skid marks and the probable place of impact. I watched an officer pick up and bag some car headlight fragments.

The EMS attendant I'd talked to earlier came over and motioned for me to get out of the car. "The A.I. asked me to tell you they called Child Services for the little girl, but it looks to be awhile. They've had a couple other emergencies."

"That's okay. I don't have any place I need to be and can stay here until they come."

"Uh, well, we still have a problem." He was short, redheaded and had freckles across his nose. He looked around twenty-five, but his hair had receded back past his ears. "The M.E. said we could go ahead and transport the woman soon, but I think it's a bad idea to do it in front of the child."

"No problem. I'll drive April to headquarters and wait for Child Services there. We'll go now, and you can take care of things."

"Good, I was hoping you'd say that."

I got back into the car and saw that April had indeed cried herself to sleep. I pulled the seat belt around her and fastened it. My car engine started with hardly a sound, and I pulled slowly around the crime scene, heading west.

I intended to drive to headquarters with April. Honestly, I did. But my place was just down the road, and when I reached the driveway of my apartment complex I turned in almost automatically and pulled around to my parking space.

"Poor little kid doesn't need any more hassles tonight," I said as I turned off the ignition.

I picked up April. She was so frail her little body couldn't have weighed more than thirty pounds. Her arms tightened around my neck and she mumbled something that sounded like, "Santa Claus."

"Okay, sweetie. Don't you worry. Santa is coming to see you."

She was dead asleep again and didn't even awaken when I put her on my sofa and stripped off her soiled clothes. I got one of my T-shirts and pulled it over her head. I carried her to my bedroom and tucked her in bed. She aroused enough to put her thumb in her mouth and then she zonked.

I sat for a few moments thinking it all over before I called downtown. I knew I'd get an argument, but I stuck to my guns and in the end got what I wanted. "I promise," I said. "She'll be there on the twenty-sixth."

I slept for about three hours, and April didn't move or turn over. After I had showered I called my mother because I desperately needed her help. There was no way I could take off work as we were down to a skeleton crew already.

My parents, Helene and Herbert Taylor, live in West Lake Hills, a section of Austin noted for canyons, hills and homes with breathtaking views.

My parents aren't rich, but they would be considered comfortable. Dad has his own engineering firm, and Mom retired from the University of Texas Chancellor's office last year. They built their home years ago when prices were still reasonable. It's worth a small fortune now.

I knew my mom would say she was busy with her final preparations for a big family dinner on Christmas Eve, but I also knew everything was already done.

My mom is the great goddess of organization and never procrastinates. She just likes to make us feel sorry for her by making us think she's harried at the last minute. She complained a bit, but agreed to come over about nine.

When Helene Taylor came in, she said exactly what was on her mind. "Zoe, I don't think this is a very good idea."

"It seemed like a great one at four o'clock this morning. Mom, it's just until after Christmas."

April woke up and started calling her Mommy, and that was the end of the discussion.

When I got to work I called the traffic division to see what the latest word was on the hit and run. I was glad to discover the investigator now in charge was Trey Gerrod. He had been one of my training officers and he was a first-rate officer. After we exchanged pleasantries, he clued me in on what they'd found.

"We've got paint samples and headlight fragments, Zoe. The car was identified as a 1991 Buick. Metallic Blue."

"I suppose there are only ten thousand of those around."

"Yes, but we got lucky. It had been repainted recently, and that means it was probably in an earlier accident. We'll be able to narrow it down soon."

He said they'd not identified April or her mother yet, and I mentioned my plans about calling a news reporter friend to help. He said he'd been considering that idea, too, and for me to go ahead if I had a connection.

"Keep me posted, would you?" I asked.

"Okay. Hey, is it true the little girl is staying with you?"

"Well, just until after Christmas."

"Great. Is it okay if a few of the guys around here get her some Christmas presents?"

Tough cops? They're the biggest bunch of old softies when it comes to kids. "Sure. Y'all want to stop by to-night?"

"It's a deal," he said and we hung up.

My newspaper friend worked at *The Austin American*

Statesman. Mildred Warner and I had been in some classes together at Austin Community College about a hundred years ago. She might be off for the holidays, I thought, as I dialed, but she answered her phone. "Millie, Zoe Barrow. Merry Christmas."

"Zoe? Long time no hear from. Ho, ho, ho, to you too."

When I explained the situation she was more than willing to photograph April and run a "Do You Know This Child?" article on her. We set up a late afternoon appointment at my house.

Paperwork kept me occupied for the next two hours, and then it was time to hit some parties. Christmas is when each department at HPD holds open house. Food, I never saw such good food: cookies, candies, spice and fruit cakes, banana nut and cranberry breads and muffins, huge trays of turkey, shrimp, roast beef and ham, cheeses, dips, chips, veggie and relish trays, no-nog eggnog and punch. It was pig-out time—just for the holiday, you understand—and I ate until I nearly got sick.

When I got home, Mom and April were getting along like old chums. April, brown hair brushed and curling a bit on top and with an occasional smile on her face, was a totally different child. Although there was still a trace of a haunted look in her fawn-like eyes.

Mom had taken the child shopping and bought a whole wardrobe of clothes—shoes, underwear—and to top it off, a small Christmas tree. April spent five minutes telling me how much fun they had decorating.

"She's a sweetie," Helene said. "She's been brought up right." That was the highest praise my mother could bestow.

My mom is great with little ones. My brother Chip and his wife Pat have two: Kyle, 3 and Alicia, 6. They stay with my folks on occasion and always have the greatest time.

Millie Warner came by and got the information for the article she planned to run on Christmas Day, then her photographer showed up and we had a small crisis when April decided she didn't want her picture taken. Mom finally convinced April by showing her photos in an album of me at age four and five.

My younger brother and I always played pranks on each other. One picture showed me all dressed up in Easter finery and my brother sneaking up behind the chair; just as the picture was snapped, Chip stuck his fingers up so it looked like I had horns on my head. Mom said it was entirely appropriate, because I often was a little devil, and April got so tickled she forgot she didn't want to sit still and pose.

Millie and the photographer left, and my mom took off soon after, getting my promise that April and I would spend tomorrow night with her and my dad.

The doorbell rang a few minutes later. When I answered Santa Claus stood on the front stoop with five uniformed police officers instead of elves, each holding a gaily wrapped present.

"April, look who's here. Someone special has come to see you."

I saw her out of the corner of my eye as she edged across the living room, but when she caught sight of the man in the red suit, April suddenly began screaming and ran down the hall to the bedroom.

"Why is she having such a fit? Is this kid strange or what?" I looked at the group, two women and three men, and said, "Sorry, guys. Come on in and sit. I'll go and see what I can do with her."

Santa, or rather Trey Gerrod dressed in the suit, said,

"Take it easy, Zoe. Lots of little kids are afraid of Santa."

"Younger kids maybe, but a four-year-old?"

"Kids are all different. My five-year-old daughter still cries when she sees him—she doesn't scream, but she cries. My son, who is three, runs to him laughing, all excited to sit in Santa's lap."

"Okay, maybe I should just leave her alone a minute." I poured coffee and got some of my mom's fudge and divinity candy out for my guests. They put the presents they'd brought around the tree.

I told Trey about Millie's article, and he said he hoped it worked. They sure didn't have anything on April's mother. All the while we talked her screams grew louder. I finally gave up and walked down the hall to the bedroom.

"April, honey? This isn't a very nice way to act. Come to the living room with me; we'll have some candy and talk to Santa."

"I no want any canny," she said, between sobs. "I want my mommy. Where's my mommy?"

It wasn't going to be easy. My mom had told April this morning that her mommy had gone to live in heaven and that we couldn't go there right now. I tried to explain things again, but she was too young to understand. I felt totally inadequate.

Since I'd never had children, I knew much less about kids than most women my age. I couldn't help wondering if I'd made a big mistake by bringing this little girl home with me.

Finally she stopped crying and stuck her thumb in her mouth. She still didn't want to go out to see Santa, so I left her lying on my bed, watching Sesame Street and hugging the teddy bear she got last night.

When I returned to the living room, the little group had

already left, all except Santa. Trey Gerrod made a great St. Nick as he was on the roly-poly side, with round cheeks and blue eyes. He didn't have a beard though and had to wear the false whiskers.

He filled me in on the progress they'd made in identifying the hit and run vehicle. "We've narrowed it to three cars. All have been in the shop in the past eight to ten months for paint jobs. We've talked to the owners and all of them have good alibis."

"What about the cars? What about damage?"

"No damage to two of them, but the third car has left town. Which sounds a little suspicious to me. The owner, a Mr. Randall Lack, says his son took the Buick this morning to drive to Fort Worth to visit his mother. The parents are divorced, and the son lives with his father."

"And you think this could be the one?"

"It's only a guess. However, Lack does have the strongest alibi. He was at a Christmas party and seen by about fifty people." Trey smiled. "He played Santa and wore a suit and everything. Can you imagine a grown man acting that way?"

I eyed Trey and realized his tongue was planted firmly in his cheek. "No, I can't imagine it. So, Lack was there all evening?"

"He supposedly left around midnight to go home, and we haven't proved otherwise yet."

"So there's not . . ."

"We haven't given up, Zoe. I'm not called 'tenacious' for nothing." He smiled, and I'd have sworn his blue eyes twinkled. "I need to head on down the avenue. We're taking our kids to my mom and dad's tonight. Tomorrow we go to Sara's folks."

I walked with him to the door. "Thanks, Trey. Tell the

others they were sweet to come, and I appreciate the presents. I'm sorry April didn't get into the spirit."

"No problem. She's been through a lot, and it's going to take a bunch of love to get her back on track."

As I closed the door behind Trey I thought about what he'd said. He was right. April would need a lot of love. Someone to care for her unconditionally. Someone to love her as much as their own. I knew her immediate fate was to be sent to a foster home. Would they be capable of giving her the love she needed?

I grilled a couple of chicken breasts, made a salad, cooked some rice and opened a package of brown gravy mix. My mind kept walking around the idea of what it would be like to be a mother. It did have a certain appeal, I admitted, but a kid with so many problems would be a handful. Even I could figure that one.

Byron and I had talked about having kids. Sometime in the future maybe, we'd say, but not yet. We'll get around to it. We hadn't known then his future was limited. The doctors say he'll never wake up from his coma, and he and I will never have the family we talked about. Now I'd never be a mother.

When I went to see if April was ready to eat she'd gone to sleep. It didn't surprise me. She'd worn herself out with her emotional outburst. She'd not slept much last night, and since she and my mother had run around half the day shopping, sleep was inevitable. No wonder the little thing got the screaming meemies. She was worn to a frazzle.

After all the stuff I'd eaten earlier at the office, I realized I wasn't hungry either, so I wrapped things up and put them in the refrigerator. I decided to take a warm bubble bath and afterwards, climbed in bed to read. I'm not too crazy about police and crime books—they're usually either

too realistic or not realistic enough, but I'd recently discovered a writer who writes about a female police chief in the
fictional town of Maggody, Arkansas, who has the knack of
tickling my funny bone. I'd just bought a recent paperback
and was looking forward to it.

Around nine p.m., April woke up wanting something to
eat. We raced to the kitchen, I let her win, and on the lower
shelf of the pantry, I found a can of chicken noodle soup.
Mom must have bought because it wasn't anything I usually
stocked. I heated the soup in the microwave, and April got
a spoon and some crackers out even though it wasn't too
easy seeing as how she had a teddy bear in one arm. I
dished up some of the salad I'd made earlier for myself.

"Are you feeling better now?" I asked as she began
eating.

"Jay..es." She almost smiled and took a drink of milk,
leaving a mustache of white above her lip.

"I'm glad. Did you and Mo . . ." I broke off. I knew what
my brother's kids called Mom, but didn't know what she'd
told April to call her. "Did you and Mamma-lene go buy
groceries?"

"Jay..es."

"Good, can you say yes?"

"Yes." This time she did smile, lighting up her whole
face.

"Very good, April." She was a cutie and would be even
cuter with a little meat on her bones. "After you finish
eating we'll go turn on the Christmas tree lights. Would you
like that?"

"Yes." She finished the soup and asked for more.

It was good to see her eating so well, even if it was an
odd time for dinner. While April ate the additional soup, I

looked in the refrigerator and pantry to see what extra goodies Mom had bought. I found a carton of Blue Bell Ice Cream—Buttered Pecan—my favorite. April and I each had some.

We finished the ice cream, I washed her face and hands, and we walked to the living room where I turned on the tree lights. When the lights started blinking off and on, April clapped her hands in glee.

"You're a lucky little girl, April. Look at all these presents with your name on them. Look at what Santa Claus brought for you."

April started screaming again, but this time she ran to me and put her arms around my legs, almost toppling me. Not easy when you're five feet nine like I am. She's frightened, I thought. "Honey, what's wrong? What are you afraid of?"

"That Santa Claus."

"You're afraid of Santa?"

"Jay..es."

Maybe if I was used to little kids I'd have snapped to it sooner, but now at least the light was beginning to dawn. "Why are you afraid of Santa? Did Santa hurt you?"

"No, he hurt Mommy."

"How did Santa hurt your mommy?"

"Mommy said, 'NO, NO.' He pushed her. Mommy fall out. Mommy cried."

"Santa pushed your mommy out of the car?" I needed to know if they had been inside the car. If they had, it would open up the possibilities and help make the case.

"Jay..es. Mommy told me run. I run. Mommy run. Santa's big car hit Mommy." Tears welled up in her eyes.

I changed the subject. I didn't want her thinking about the bad part right now. "Santa took you for a ride in his car?"

"J..yes. We go to Old McDonald's. And I got french fries."

"Do you like french fries?"

"Yes, with ketchup."

"I like french fries and ketchup too. Maybe we can go to McDonald's tomorrow and get french fries. I think it's time now for us to go to bed."

"Okay." She took my hand and led me down the hallway.

We held hands until she went to sleep. Maybe being a parent wasn't so difficult after all.

Thinking over my talk with April, I began to get a mental picture of what must have happened to her and her mom. The picture was still fuzzy, but it was a likely scenario which explained why April was afraid of anyone dressed as Santa.

A man dressed in a Santa suit had picked them up someplace. Trey Gerrod had mentioned one of his metallic blue car owners had dressed as Santa—that connected up. Maybe he offered to buy them food and took them to McDonalds. Maybe he offered money for sex too, beforehand, and April's mom said okay, but feed us first. After eating maybe she wasn't so eager to go along with the sex part and refused to give him whatever he wanted.

That refusal made him angry, and he shoved them out of his car. Maybe she taunted him or mouthed off at him. Whatever, his anger exploded, and he ran the mother down. The idea was feasible, and the best part from the police point of view was that April and her mom were in that vehicle. Some trace of hair or fiber could turn up in the car.

I'd thrown away the clothing April had worn; nothing had been worth salvaging. Tomorrow I'd dig them out of the garbage can and take them to the forensics lab for testing.

116

★ ★ ★ ★ ★

First thing the next morning, I called my sister-in-law to ask if I could bring April to her house while I was at work.

"No," said Pat. "Helene said for me to tell you to bring April to her house. She knew you'd hesitate to ask her help today."

"But she's got . . ."

"You know she's got everything done."

"I just thought April would enjoy playing with Alicia and Kyle."

"I'll be at your mom's most of the day, and we can manage three between us."

"Sound like you two have things all arranged."

Pat and Helene get along well as Pat is almost as good an organizer as my mom. They gave up on me a long time ago. I'm okay at work, but in most everything else, I'm usually disorganized. Sometimes I envy Pat and her relationship with Helene, but she will often side with me, keeping Mom off my back. Besides, I liked her.

"Okay," I said. "I'll take April over there, and thanks for your help."

A Canadian cold front had moved down across the Texas plains and into central Texas overnight. Made it feel more like Christmas to be able to put on a jacket. Mom had bought a coat with a hood for April, and she got so excited I wondered if the kid had ever had one before.

After I dropped April at Mom's, I dropped April's clothes at the lab at headquarters and headed to the East Station patrol building off East 7th to talk with Trey Gerrod. I found him in his lieutenant's office finishing up a telephone call. When I told him what April had said, he got a funny look on his face.

"I just talked to the M.E.," Trey said. "April's mother

had sex as recently as two hours before her death. I was getting ready to start looking for a boyfriend or a pimp."

"Or a customer?"

"That too. It had occurred to me she was killed by some weirdo or a disgruntled John." He leaned back in the chair and looked at me through narrowed eyes. "If she had sex with the guy, why did he get mad and run her down?"

"Who knows? Like you said, a weirdo with a weirdo reason."

"We know that Mr. Lack was dressed in a Santa suit."

"Right," I said.

He picked up the Austin telephone directory. "Do you want in on this?"

"You bet your buns."

Gerrod handed me the directory. "Look up the locations for all the McDonalds, and we'll go talk to some civilians."

I contacted my boss, who gave me a green light to stay with the case. "Nothing except more parties going on around here," he said.

"Save some goodies for me."

He promised he would, and when I'd hung up the phone, I flipped open the directory. "Good grief, Trey. There are seventeen McDonalds here. I had no idea there were so many."

"We only need the ones within 2–3 miles of East Riverside Drive."

I studied the addresses a moment. "That leaves four, East Ben White, East Oltorf, Barton Springs and East Riverside Drive. But the Riverside one is probably too far east, and the one on William Cannon is probably too far south."

"Let's try those first three," he said. "We can move farther out if nothing turns up in one of those."

After a brief argument about who was going to drive,

Trey and I left in my Mustang. It was his case, but I remembered riding patrol with him years ago. He drove like a little old country farmer, and that drove me crazy. We reached I-35 and headed south. "If you had to guess, Trey, where do you like best?"

"I like the Barton Springs location. He probably picked them up in the downtown area or near Zilker Park."

I had thought the Ben White location for the easy access to I-35, but Trey made a good point. "Okay, let's go there first."

"You're driving," he said.

"Yeah, I remember Santa and the little girl," the young man said. "They pulled up to the window about 12:30 or 1:00 last night."

The hamburger emporium's night manager was working again this fine Christmas Eve morning. Guess McDonalds was on a skeleton crew, too. Trey and I ordered coffee and sat in the booth nearest the counter. The manager, Bob Cortez, was in his early thirties, short and thin, and had an Adam's apple that looked like he'd actually swallowed an apple. He sat beside me, keeping an eye on his three other workers.

"That's the same little girl in today's paper, isn't it?" he asked. "I was pretty sure it was her." One of the girls from the kitchen called for Cortez, sounding like it might be a major calamity, and he said he'd be right back.

"April's in the paper today? I thought it was going to run tomorrow—Christmas Day." Trey shrugged and I said, "I didn't have time to even look at the newspaper this morning."

"Have a little trouble being a mother, did you?"

"It's not easy getting a kid and yourself bathed, dressed,

fed and out the door on time. Especially when you're not used to it." I could smile now, but this morning I wanted to tear out my hair. "April didn't want to wear the blue jeans I put on her. She wanted to wear the red corduroy pants today."

Trey laughed. "So, who won?"

"She looked cute in the red. It seemed too trivial to fuss about, but I had to take off the jeans and put on the corduroys because we were going to be late if I let her do it."

"You'll soon figure out how to work it."

"You're talking like she's going to stay with me. This is only temporary."

"I hear you. I just don't believe you." Trey pulled the front page section of the paper out of his jacket pocket and handed it to me.

While I was reading the article Millie had done, Cortez came back, apologetic.

"No problem," said Trey. "Tell us what you remember."

Cortez remembered the car, the woman and the child, but especially he recalled the man. "Someone dressed like Santa is hard to forget."

"Did he have on the full costume?" I asked.

"Everything except the whiskers."

"Did you get a good look at him?" asked Trey.

Cortez nodded. "Dark hair, young, maybe about twenty. That struck me as a little odd. I figured he was the younger brother or something and had done this for the little girl."

When Cortez had nothing more to add, Trey and I walked out to my car.

"None of my blue Buick owners were young," said Trey.

"But one of them had a son old enough to drive."

"Mr. Lack," said Trey. "Let's go see old Randall Lack. Maybe he'll tell us why his son really drove up to Ft. Worth the next morning after a hit and run."

It was routine after that. Mr. Lack didn't want to cooperate until Trey Gerrod mentioned the Fort Worth police had Randall, Jr., in custody. A search warrant had been obtained for the car.

Lack finally admitted his son had told him that he'd put on the Santa suit and had gone out to play a joke on his friends. Lack denied any knowledge about the hit and run.

I let Trey handle things from that point and drove over to my parents' house. Millie Warner called to say several people had called the *Statesman* saying they knew April and her mother. No one knew of any other family. April's last name was Collins, and her mother's name was Reba. The newspaper was starting a fund for April and was also donating a funeral for Reba Collins.

My family, including aunts, uncles and cousins, had all fallen for April, and she was responding to their care and concern. Everyone kept asking me what was I going to do? Hell, I didn't know.

Later that evening, I slipped away from all the family festivities and drove to the nursing home to visit Byron. As I sat in the car outside the building housing my comatose husband, I was still unsure that what I wanted to do was the right thing for me or for April.

The night was clear, and you could see millions of stars, bright and twinkling in the black sky. High wispy clouds were visible against the inky velvet, looking as if an artist had painted them there only a few minutes earlier.

Christmas is a time for giving and receiving love. Love was something a child could bring into my lonely life. I got out of the car and automatically looked upward to see if I could spot a miniature sleigh or Rudolph and eight tiny reindeer.

"Byron," I said aloud in the crisp night air. "Guess what Santa brought me for Christmas?"

Kittens Take Detection 101

She lived in my neighborhood and looked a bit wrinkled, maybe slightly shopworn around the edges. Her dark hair was lightly streaked with gray. You couldn't tell her age, but you never doubted for a minute someone might call her grandmother. Most people probably wouldn't look at her twice. Her grandson later said she had been born mildly retarded, but I think her mental processes worked fine except for a minor slowing. Delilah Miller was her name, and I wished I'd been a better neighbor.

For a time after my husband Tommy had been killed, I had leased out our house and lived in an apartment, but this past summer I decided I wanted back in my house. Besides, apartment rents in Austin kept skyrocketing. With the help of friends I renovated and redecorated until nothing remained as it had been. I had fallen in love with the house when Tommy and I had bought it all those years ago, and I enjoyed living in it once again. The older neighborhood with large trees, flowers and plush lawns reflected a settled and perhaps friendly place. And friendly it has become for me.

I had noticed my neighbor who lived on the corner almost every morning for several weeks as I power-walked around my neighborhood and always waved to her. Sometimes I stopped, especially when she offered fresh vegetables from her garden. I didn't stop often, however, because she liked to tell you about her grandson who was a Master Chef at some fancy hotel restaurant in Houston, and it was the same story every time. She obviously forgot she'd already told you before. And it was difficult to get away once you stopped, but she enjoyed the company when I did stop.

Recent cool rainy days, not exactly normal for autumn in central Texas but no doubt brought on by El Niño, had shortened my walks or even halted them. I didn't see Delilah during that time, but didn't think much about it because of the weather. But when the rain stopped and sunny fall weather came back and I still didn't see her, I wondered. She stayed on the edges of my mind, yet it was another three days before I stopped to ask.

"She went to visit her sister in Oklahoma City," her grandson said. He looked as if he'd never eaten a fattening meal in his life. His skin was pasty white, and his blue eyes were pale and listless. "She's even thinking of moving up there. Says she wants to be close to someone of her own age."

"Probably a good idea," I said. "I just worried she might be sick."

The grandson had yelled out that he wasn't buying when I rang the doorbell. After I explained who I was and what I wanted, he'd peeked out, then opened only a little wider when he saw me, but kept his foot against it as if to keep me from shoving my way past him.

"I appreciate your asking," he said in a solemn tone, then abruptly closed the front door and left me standing on the porch, wondering if I should ring the bell again.

Maybe it was my imagination, but as I stood there looking at that closed door, all the short hair on the back of my neck rose up. He was lying through his teeth, but I had no idea why I knew that was so.

Of course I admit to being nosy, but what gave him the right to be rude? My nosy nature stood me well in both of my life's careers.

My first career had been as a radiological technologist, a high falutin' name for a diagnostic X-ray tech where my curiosity centered on how the body worked and what went where. My second career, as a private investigator, became much more intriguing and one I now enjoyed. Being nosy was a definite plus.

I left my neighbor's porch and walked briskly to my place. When I got inside, Nick and Nora greeted me like I'd been gone for a week instead of the forty-five minutes it had taken to walk my four miles. "Hey, guys. Did you miss me?" They both meowed how they thought I'd deserted them and how could I be so cruel?

When I moved from my apartment, I left Sam Spade with my neighbor, Glenda Knipstein, who had found him originally. He knew and liked her, and it didn't seem fair to move him from the area where he'd lived all his five years. Older cats don't accept change very well. Spade had fathered a litter in the spring, and I couldn't imagine a home without a cat. The little ones were ready to be weaned shortly before I moved, and I wound up with two kittens, one male and one female. Two would be able to keep each other company, I thought. Little did I know two also meant double trouble. Because their father had been named Sam Spade, I'd called him Spade for short, and I decided appropriate names for the babies should be Nick and Nora. The cats were not a specific breed, but had the look of the chocolate Burmese.

The black balls of fur beat me to the bedroom where I stripped off my sweats and turned on the hot water in the shower. I closed the kittens out of the bathroom—they liked to lick the water from my legs when I get out and their sandpaper tongues could tickle.

"does she really think we miss her?" nick said as the kittens

settled down outside the door. she put a paw underneath and pulled, hoping the door would open. nick sat trying to figure out how the door worked—somehow it managed to baffle him.

"of course not, that's just the way she talks. haven't you got used to it yet?"

"well, i have better things to do with my time." he strolled over to the bedroom trash basket, stood up with his paws on the top edge and looked inside. "hey, here's one of those popping things . . . oh yeah, she called it a rubber band. these are great fun to play with." he pulled the band out and began batting it around. "see, i told you i was too busy to miss mamma jenny." (the human female brought them here when they were nine weeks old, and they knew she wasn't their mother but they hadn't known anything else to call her except mamma jenny.)

nora kept thinking about how mamma jenny's face looked. "something is bothering her."

"what do you mean? she looks the same to me."

nora hopped upon the bed. "no. she's got that frown between her eyes. i've seen her look that way before, and when it's there she's worried about something."

nick jumped on the bed, grabbed nora around the neck and began licking her ear. "you're always so observant. but who cares if she's worried? she is human, and that's something i've noticed they do a lot."

"i care. she's a nice human companion, and i want to stay here with her," nora said, pushing him away. she hopped off the bed. "besides, i want to learn to be a private investigator like her and uncle louie. if she's worried about a case maybe i can help."

"that's about the dumbest idea you've ever had." nick jumped up on the dresser and looked inside a little velvet box. he found a pair of shiny ball objects with some wires on one end and some dangle gewgaws on the other. he knocked one of them to the floor.

both kittens pounced on the object and began batting and chasing it around the room. nick's favorite game was "keep away."

"why is that dumb?"

"because you're a cat."

"i know i'm a cat, brother, and that's why i'd be really good at this. i'm curious, i'm resourceful, i'm intelligent. uncle louie is an ace detective, and i want to be just like him. i've read stories about his cases." midnight louie was a direct uncle on their father's side.

nick swished a doubtful tail in her direction.

"if you think cats can't read you're sadly mistaken. uncle louie says we don't read words line by line, but we absorb the whole pages by sitting on them or under them or around them. i've already learned, and i'm sure you will soon too."

"you're nuts," nick said. he started chasing nora, but since he was twice her size, she was too quick for him. she ran down the hall and into the kitchen, hiding in the shadows of the dining table. in a while he gave up and sauntered back into the bedroom and soon hopped up on the bed, wetting his paw and washing his ear. to heck with them both, he thought. when his ears felt clean enough he curled up in a ball and went to sleep. nora returned to the bedroom in a few minutes, saw her brother was asleep and sat down to wait for mamma jenny.

after jenny got out of the shower and dressed, nora kept watching and wondering why her human mom was worried.

maybe if i get in her lap she'll talk to me and i'll find out what the problem is. nora jumped up on the dresser, walked over and looked deep into the human's eyes. she knew sometimes she and the female person almost made a mental connection.

"Hey, little one," said Jenny. "What are you up to?" She picked up the earring Nick had sent skittering across the floor earlier. "Nick really likes shiny things, doesn't he?"

She turned, dropped the earring back into its box and put the lid on tight. She spoke again to Nora, then looked around for Nick. "Oh. I see. Your brother is asleep and you want some company. Come up here. I'll pet you."

Jenny placed the kitten over her left forearm, with all four of Nora's legs dangling on either side of her arm. She headed to her favorite overstuffed chair in the family room, taking the morning newspaper with her.

Minutes later the phone rang. The noise startled Nora, but Jenny kept petting the kitten as she answered. "Hello? Oh, hi, C.J." Jenny listened for a moment.

"Things are slow here. Boring. Now tell me what a great time you're having in Hawaii." She listened and giggled. "He didn't! He danced the hula to a whole song up on stage?" She laughed heartily this time. "I'd like to have seen that."

Jenny's partner C.J. had gone to Hawaii for a Private Eye convention.

boring right here now, too, thought nora and dropped back off to sleep.

"No need for you to hurry back. Nothing exciting's happening. Stay another week if you want to . . . No way. I wouldn't be mad. Nope. C.J., I'm serious. Take all the time you like. But next time I get to go, and you stay home and work. Just hope it's someplace that's fun." One year the convention was in Houston. A fun town, but one too familiar.

They exchanged more small talk and some business talk. Then Jenny said, "I am a little distracted. My neighbor— you remember Mrs. Miller? I missed seeing her for a few days, and when I stopped to ask about her this morning, her grandson nearly bit my head off."

nora woke up and listened. so that's what's been on her

mind. nick and i need to find a way outside and go to mrs.
miller's house. i've seen a big gray and white cat living near
there. maybe he knows something and maybe he's friendly. nora
listened long enough to be sure she wasn't missing more impor-
tant information then went back to sleep.

That night I didn't sleep well. I kept dreaming about
Delilah Miller and the dreams were not good. By the next
morning I convinced myself to dig a bit deeper into the situation.

Austin sits atop an unusual geographic area even for
Texas. An old fault line known as the Balcones Fault runs
along the western edge. The east side of the city slopes into
gentle rolling hills while the western side shifts into canyons
and limestone bluffs. If that's not unusual enough, the
Texas Colorado River (not the same one found in the
Grand Canyon) meanders through the town. Most of the
commercial part of downtown lies on the North bank of the
river. The river has been dammed many times from the hill
country on its way to the Gulf of Mexico in an effort to con-
tain the water and utilize it. A chain of lakes formed from
the dams, and the area is well known as a recreation and
living area. The nine lakes in the chain are known as the
Highland Lakes.

We're close enough to the Gulf Coast to be subject to
warm moist tropical air sweeping north, which then collides
with the cold invading Canadian air. Consequently we're
often hampered with heavy patches of fog like today. The
fog left misty crud on my windshield and gave all lights an
almost surreal hazy ring. The gray day matched my mood as
I drove the few blocks to work.

Our fourth floor office in the LaGrange building always
seemed dark and empty without C.J. Besides being my
partner she was also my best friend. I pushed the door with

its discrete sign reading G. & G. Investigations, closed it and called our answering service. No messages, they said.

I'll never be too good at operating computers as I flunked mechanical ability in kindergarten and never recovered, but C.J. did teach me a few tricks. Like looking up addresses on the Internet. I remembered Delilah mentioning once that her sister had never married and their maiden name was Bayliss. I found a Marilee Bayliss in Oklahoma City on Drakestone Avenue with a phone number listed.

There was no answer when I called, but an answering machine asked me to leave a message so I did. About an hour later when the telephone rang, a low alto voice asked for Jenny Gordon.

"This is she," I said.

"I'm Marilee Bayliss. My sister isn't here. Whatever gave you the idea that she was?"

"The young man in her house . . . her grandson, isn't he? He told me Mrs. Miller left a few days ago to come and visit you."

"Oh, my. Grady said that? I wonder why that boy lied? Well, I guess that's not too unusual. He always did tell more lies than not—even when he was a teensy tyke. I haven't seen or heard from Delilah in a good week. Let me think a minute now. Okay, I went to choir practice last Tuesday night—I sing in the choir at Second Baptist—and I spoke with her just before I left here. In fact, I've been getting a little worried about her since I haven't been able to reach her by telephone. I called last Sunday. We nearly always talk on Sundays because the rates are cheaper." She paused a moment to breathe and continued. "I don't know what Grady's doing in her house anyway. He's supposed to be at that fancy hotel restaurant job of his working, I would think. Unless he's taking some vacation time or something.

129

But for him to say Delilah is up here with me is an out and out lie."

"Do you know any place else Mrs. Miller might go?" She asked me to call her Marilee.

"Goodness no. No place that I can think of. And now you've got me worried," she said. "Do you think I should report her missing to the police, Jenny?"

"Let me make some inquiries first, Miss Bayliss. Maybe she got sick and had to go to the hospital."

"But surely Delilah would call. Or the hospital would. I'm listed as her next of kin for emergencies." She took another breath, and her voice got higher. "Oh my, oh my. I'm scared something bad has happened to her. But why hasn't Grady called to tell me? Maybe I'll call and ask him what's going on. No. Maybe I'd better come down there and see to things myself."

"Miss Bayliss, uh . . . Marilee, try to be calm for a moment. I can think of several reasons for Mrs. Miller to be gone, and Grady could be house sitting for her. He probably only told me she was at your place just to get rid of me since I was being a nosy neighbor." I didn't really think so, but didn't want to worry Miss Bayliss anymore than she already was. "Let me check around, Marilee, and I'll call you back later today."

"What would you charge to investigate?"

"There's no charge. Mrs. Miller's a neighbor and friend. Besides, what I'll do only takes a few phone calls."

I spent the rest of the morning calling area hospitals, including the bedroom communities of Round Rock, Georgetown, New Braunfels and San Marcos. I even called Scott & White, a large medical facility in Temple about an hour north of Austin, but one well known, Many people around the state go there. Then to be on the safe side I called the medical examiner's office to see if they had a Jane Doe fitting Delilah Miller's description. My final call was to the Austin Police Department's Missing Persons. Each response was negative, and by now my suspicions were increasing that this grandson of Delilah's had done something with his grandmother. It wasn't a pleasant thought.

My late husband was a police officer before he resigned to open a private detective office, and I have a few friends still there from those old days. I persuaded one pal, Linda Cooper from narcotics, into pulling the rap sheet on one Gradon Lee Miller a.k.a. Grady Miller.

"I'll call you back tomorrow morning," Linda said.

"I'll buy you a steak tonight at The Outback if you can have some information for me then."

"Is seven too early?" she wanted to know.

"Perfect. See you then."

Without C.J. around I sure didn't want to stay in this lonesome office until it got dark, so I left a little after the noon hour. I stopped for cat food and a huge sack of litter before heading home.

Nick and Nora heard the garage door open and met me at the door leading from the garage to the kitchen. "Hey, guys," I said. "What's happening? Look, I got a new big sack of yummy kitten chow for you."

"And," I said, "I saved the best part till last. Ta-da." I held out the litter sack. "Fresh odor-free scoopable stuff for your box." They both yawned and stretched and strolled over to their food dishes.

"well, la-di-dah," said nick.

"boy, are you going to be grumpy all day?" nora asked. "you're always the first one to complain. but when things are top-notch, do you ever act appreciative?"

"don't i let her pet me? don't i sleep curled up at the foot of

her bed every night? okay. sorry. remember i'm in my teen-age years and am prone to being moody and ill-tempered."

"that's no excuse. you must think whining or complaining is cute or something. believe me, it's not."

"okay, i said, i'm sorry." nick bounded away and thought to himself, she's just jealous because i hid my new toy and she can't find it. usually she finds everything i hide, but i have a new place she hasn't located yet, and she can't stand it. he hummed little noises as he hurried into the family room and looked inside the flower pot. yep. it's still there.

nora sat quietly pretending to eat but watching her brother the whole time. of course, he gives everything away by those little noises he makes, she thought. he nosed around the flower pot, and then sauntered off nonchalantly. so that's where his new hidey-hole is. good. in a few minutes when he's forgotten all about it, i'll go get the bauble with the black strings and hide it where he'll never find it.

nick had found the little shiny toy when they were outside exploring. mamma jenny wasn't too keen on them being outside— afraid they'd get lost or run over or something. they had gone through the cat door leading out to the garage, and nora once again found the box that opened the garage door. it was an old box, small and rather plain but magical.

the box lay up on a shelf near the top of the garage. mamma jenny probably thought they couldn't jump up that high, but nora had found she could jump up on the big washer box and then it was only a short leap to the top shelf. when she put her foot in just the right place on the little box the garage door opened. if she waited a moment and put her foot in the same spot, the door stopped again leaving an opening then large enough for both of them to slink under, yet it would stay open so they could get back into the garage. of course since nick was getting so big, she'd had to leave a bigger opening.

after mamma jenny left for work and after both kittens had taken a nap they had gone outside looking for the gray and white cat who lived near the corner house.

"hi," *nora said to him when she found him snoozing under a tomato plant in the garden.* "i'm nora and my brother's name is nick. we live over there," *she said, pointing her nose in the direction of their house.* "do you live here?"

naturally he and nick had to smell each other first, and then hiss a little before finally deciding their age difference was sufficient to let them be friends rather than enemies.

"no. i live next door. my name is bing clawsby"

"hi, bing. do you know that lady who lives here?"

"sure, mrs. miller. but i haven't see her in several days."

bing had a nice melodious purr and voice. "i wonder if she's gone on vacation or something. that man-child who's there now is mean. he keeps chasing me out of the garden here, but it's a wonderful place to nap. the dirt is soft and cool under some of these plants. mrs. miller never cared if i slept here." *he walked to another plant and began scratching.* "someone was digging in this dirt not long ago and it's very easy to hallow out a nice spot for napping."

"yes. i can see how nice it is," *said nick. he kept walking around and found a spot that smelled quite pungent to him. he began scratching the dirt and pushing it aside. that's when he found the shiny bauble with black strings hanging from it.*

"hey don't use my sleeping places for a bathroom," *said bing. he didn't notice what nick was playing with.*

"aw, come on," *said nick.* "i have better manners. we use a litter box indoors anyway."

"sorry, didn't mean anything. guess i'm not used to youngsters anymore. you guys still are kittens, aren't you?"

"sure are," *said nora as she checked to see what nick was doing. she couldn't tell for sure, but it looked as if he had some-*

thing in his mouth. "we won't be a year old for three more months." she'd overheard mamma jenny tell some friend how old they were on the telephone the other day. she saw nick pick up his treasure and turn to head home. "well, i guess we'll go now," she told bing. "we aren't actually supposed to be outside, and we'd better get back."

"probably a good idea," agreed bing. he obviously hadn't been too sure that nick hadn't messed up his napping spots.

nora didn't get a chance to get to the toy from nick's hiding place because mamma jenny came home earlier than expected.

As usual in central Texas, the sun burned off the fog and the day had shaped up quite nicely. I'd had no luck locating Mrs. Miller either as a patient or a corpse. Which was a relief in a way. Except I needed to think about what I was going to tell Marilee Bayliss. She'd probably want to come down, and maybe that was best. Maybe Grady Miller would be obliged then to tell her where her sister had gone.

After a late lunch and changing clothes I decided to move some plants out to the patio to catch a few rays. Soon it will be too cold, and they'll have to stay indoor for days on end. I knew I was putting off calling Marilee but promised myself when I had the plants situated I'd telephone her.

When I picked up the small Ficus plant I saw a shiny gold colored object half-buried in the dirt. "What's this?" I asked Nick and Nora who pretended not to hear and didn't even look in my direction.

"Damn Sam," I mumbled. "It's a watch." And as unbelievable as it seemed, this watch looked exactly like the watch Delilah Miller had worn. An old-fashioned one with black bands made of a sort of elastic cord.

"damn sam," echoed nora. "she found your treasure."

"i saw. what do you think we should do?"

"do? nothing. we'll just have to take our punishment."

"punishment? for what? we didn't do nothing."

"Okay, guys," I said. "Where did you get this watch?"

The kittens blinked innocent eyes and said nothing.

"Look," I said. "I know this watch wasn't here last night because I checked the soil to see if it needed water." The kittens yawned and stretched and played dumb.

"Nora, what worries me is the lady who owns this watch is missing. And I'm very worried about her."

I looked closer at the watch and notice the caked mud against the stem of the watch. "Well, maybe it was in the flower pot all night," I told Nora. "It must have been there when I watered it this morning and that's how it got muddy. Also I can't imagine how you got Mrs. Miller's watch or even how you got out of the house."

Nora jumped into my lap and looked me square in the eyes. I'd swear that she could talk if she could only figure the proper sequence, but I didn't know exactly what she might say.

As I petted Nora, Nick strolled into the kitchen to his food bowl. I could hear him munching and the little noises he made sounded as if he wanted to talk to me, too.

The telephone rang and startled both kittens who ran like greased lightning to the bedroom. "Is this Jenny Gordon?" a familiar female voice asked.

"Yes, is this Marilee Bayliss?"

"Yes. I'm at the Austin airport—would it be too inconvenient if you came after me?"

It wasn't a total surprise. Marilee had been quite worried about her sister and the natural thing was to come to Austin and see about things herself. "Of course not. I'll be right out."

when mamma jenny had gone, nora said, "we need to go

135

back over to the house on the corner."

"nora, i'm not sure i want to. i think we got into some trouble by going over there earlier and . . ."

"nick, i'm going whether you go or not. if you want to be a chicken, that's fine with me. but i just know uncle louie wouldn't sit and bat toys around. he'd get out there and make things happen." she headed out the kitty door and jumped up to push on the little magic box and get the garage door to open.

"what can we do?" nick followed just as she knew he would.

"i haven't the foggiest, but we have to try something."

when they got back to mrs. miller's house, friendly mr. bing clawsby was nowhere to be seen.

"bing must have gone back home," nora said.

"smart guy. won't catch him out nosing around. trying to be some kind of detective. trying out some human occupation. cats are supposed to spend most of their time sunning, sleeping, eating, playing . . ."

nora headed back to the garden and the tomato plant where nick found the watch. "i told you if you wanted to stay home that was fine with me. you didn't have to come along."

"why should you have all the fun? and besides i should stay here to protect you if you get into trouble," nick said.

"you protect me? what a laugh." nora found an earring made of little white beads and dangle wires. "here's another treasure. she picked it up to show it to him.

"What are you animals doing?" A loud male voice startled the kittens.

Nora turned and streaked by the man, but Nick was slower and the man caught him. "Flipping cats. I don't want you digging in my garden." Grady followed Nora, but she was much too quick. She scampered around the corner of her house and slithered under the garage door.

Grady took Nick and locked him in the tool shed.

nora was so scared she ran and hid under the bed. she entirely forgot she hadn't closed the garage door. she didn't even realize she still had the beaded bauble in her mouth. in fact, when she finally could think again, her only worry was what the giant would do to her brother. "oh boy, are we in big trouble. mamma jenny, please come home!"

When I pulled into the driveway I noticed the garage door was not closed all the way. "That's strange."

Marilee said, "What?"

"My garage door is partially open. I'm sure I closed it when I left." The kittens were such scaredy-cats that I never worried they might dash out when the door opened. I pushed on the remote button, and the door rose up slowly. "Well, it wasn't opened enough for a person to get inside." I pulled the car inside and the door down and went into the house.

Marilee had been one surprise after another. She looked younger and prettier than Delilah, and she had a nice sense of humor. She was slender with dark eyes, but her hair had been streaked or frosted or whatever women called it these days. When I asked her why she'd never married she said, "I saw what a hard life Delilah had—waiting on Ray hand and foot. I didn't want to be a slave for anyone."

"Can't blame you for that one."

"After Ray died, Delilah still had to worry about Grady. His parents being killed in that car wreck when he was three was tragic."

"That is sad." In one small way I could relate. I'd lost my mother to cancer when I was twelve. My grandmother had helped my father raise me. I knew what it was like to lose a parent and to rely on a older person. My grandmother did indulge me, and I had a feeling Delilah did the same for Grady.

Marilee told me that she had telephoned her sister's house and that Grady had answered. "He sounded so strange and swore he didn't know where his grandmother might be. Said he hadn't seen her since last Thursday right after he arrived there."

Sounded weird, I thought as she continued.

"That's why I thought I should come to Austin."

On the drive to my house we decided to proceed with caution. Marilee would come to my house instead of going to Delilah's. I persuaded her my guest room would be better than staying in a motel someplace.

"Wonder where the kittens are?" I looked around inside then went out to the garage and didn't find them out there either. "They nearly always come to meet me," I said. I got my flashlight and headed for the bedroom. Sometimes if they get scared they will hide under the bed.

Sure enough, when I flashed the light under the bed, one pair of golden eyes flashed back green. "Nora, is that you?" The kitten made a small sound—not a meow—not even exactly catlike. "Where's Nick?"

Nora acted like she wasn't too interested in coming out, but I went to the back side of the bed and caught her front leg and tugged. She came out, and I could feel her quivering.

"What's wrong, little one?" I looked her over carefully and could find no injury. Then I noticed something in her mouth and took it from her.

"A pearl earring. It's got mud caked in the little cracks and crevices too."

"It belongs to Delilah," said Marilee. "She wore them almost all the time. Her husband, Ray, gave them to her on their twenty-fifth anniversary. They aren't real pearls, but she was so proud of them."

"There's no way this could have been in the flower pot like the watch. How did Nora get it, I wonder." I kept petting her, and she acted a bit calmer. "And what's happened to Nick?" I searched the house more thoroughly. I couldn't find him.

"I think it's time I made a phone call to a friend of mine at APD." Seeing Marilee's puzzlement I elaborated. "Austin Police Department. Lieutenant Larry Hayes who previously worked with my late husband. He's now in homicide."

That statement startled Marilee Bayliss, but she composed herself as best she could.

Larry wasn't at the office, but I reached him at home. When Larry and my husband started in the academy, they formed a bond and later were partners for ten years. Since Tommy's murder, Larry likes to look out for me much like a big brother. It works fine except when he thinks I'm out of line. Today he merely thought I might be losing it completely.

"I know it's a thin stretch, Larry, but I feel it in my gut."

"Okay, say I go along with you. We have no reason to search the house or grounds. No judge would give me a search warrant on gut feelings."

"I know you're right, but what if Marilee just knocks on the door, suitcase in hand, and demands to stay there in her sister's house? Maybe she can say if Delilah has gone off she would want her to take care of things." I could see Marilee nodding that she could do that.

"Maybe that would work," Larry agreed.

"Good. And beside all that, I'm searching for my cat. No reason I can't go in the back yard while Marilee's at the front door."

When I hung up Marilee said, "I think I have a back

door key to Delilah's house." She rummaged through her purse and came up with the key. "We traded keys years ago in case we ever needed to go inside each other's house."

"Okay, then I'll wait while you get your suitcase, and we'll just go over and you can demand to be let in. If he refuses you can use your key."

Marilee went to my guest room to get her things.

I sat down, still holding Nora and spoke softly to her, stroking her and reassuring her that everything would be fine and that we'd find Nick. "Okay, sweetie. Maybe you can help me. Since you can't talk my language and I can't talk yours, maybe you can show me what happened."

Nora looked deep into Jenny's eyes before hopping down and heading into the garage. She jumped up on the washer and then up to the top shelf. In a moment the garage door opened, but only a small amount.

"How did you . . ." I reached up and found a second remote control. "Oh I see. That explains it. Okay. You both probably went outside, and then you must have gone to Delilah Miller's house, right?" I put the kitten down. She looked around as if to say "follow me" and took off, scampering down the street till she reached the corner house, then hightailed it to the back yard.

Marilee followed me, and we followed Nora.

Grady Miller was in the back yard, digging a hole at one end of the garden. "Flipping cats. Well, I'll fix you. I'll move her where you'll never find her. Why can't you just leave well enough alone? All that scratching around here—digging her up. Smart aleck flipping cats."

"Grady?" Marilee asked. "What on earth are you doing?"

"Aunt Mari, did you know grandmother is buried out here? I don't understand why those black cats won't leave her grave alone. She was perfectly fine out here in the garden."

The strange look in his eyes told us more than we wanted to know. Grady Miller had gone mad. Something had snapped inside him, and there was no one at home inside his head anymore.

Marilee stood rooted as if growing in the garden. She began to cry. The next few hours would be a sad ordeal for her.

Larry walked up in time to see Grady hand Marilee Bayliss the shovel he'd been using. Larry led the young man over to his unmarked car and helped him into the back seat.

I didn't see any more because I'd just noticed Nora over by the door to the shed. I couldn't hear Nick, but I felt sure he was inside. Grady had probably killed my kitten. And if he had, I didn't know what I'd do to him—crazy man or not.

The door was locked, but Grady gave Larry the key when he asked for it.

I was so scared my hands were shaking, and I had trouble opening the door. Finally I got the door open and immediately saw Nick lying on his side. His eyes were closed, but I could see he was breathing. Nora had rushed in with me, and she immediately began washing Nick's face. In another moment he opened his eyes and meowed pitifully.

"took you long enough to get here," nick told nora as he stood up. he was a bit wobbly but couldn't understand why.

"it's not easy getting humans to do what you want," she told him as mamma jenny picked him up. "and i had to have her help. it would have taken me forever to figure out how to get inside that shed."

Marilee was still crying and upset, but I persuaded her to

carry Nora while I carried Nick home.

Larry called the necessary medical personnel and police crime scene, then left to take Grady to Seton Hospital for an evaluation.

I found a lump on Nick's head where Grady had conked him. After calling my vet he said the kitten probably has a concussion. "If there are no cuts or abrasions then just watch him for a few hours like you would a person. If he shows any sign of stress, then call me, and I'll meet you at my office."

Larry called later and filled me in on what he knew to this point. And I did my best to explain things to Marilee. "Of course the investigation is still going on, but Larry says Grady poisoned her with some mushrooms. He got angry with her because she wouldn't give him the money to open his own restaurant. He said he only wanted what was due to him. What he would inherit anyway."

"He was such a strange little boy I guess I'm not really surprised," she said. "After his parents were killed in that car accident and my sister took over the responsibility for him, he began acting even stranger."

"I guess when Delilah wouldn't give him any money he just snapped."

"There wasn't any money to give. Every penny she had went towards raising him."

"Wasn't there any money from his parents' death?"

"No. They didn't have any insurance and were heavily in debt. Delilah and her husband, Ray, paid off those debts. And when Ray died the little insurance money he had was what she used to put Grady through school."

"That's really sad then. He killed her for nothing."

"I wonder if he went crazy and killed her or if he killed her because he was crazy?"

"Guess we'll never know for certain." I looked around for my kittens. "I'm just glad these little guys are okay. But I'm going to have to make sure they don't get outside again. It's too dangerous out there."

later that evening, nick and nora were curled up beside mamma jenny on the sofa. "did we do good, sister?" nick asked.

"we did just fine. but we'll need to talk to uncle louie. learn his tricks for picking locks and whatnot and how he convinced his human to let him roam outside." nora cleaned her brother's face once again. "hmmm," she said. "wonder if there's a feline junior g-man badge or something we can get?"

I looked at my kittens. "You guys did such a great job. I'll have to declare you official cat detectives and put you on the payroll. Wonder how much shrimp and fish to pay you each week?"

"what's a shrimp and fish?" asked nora.

"who knows?" said nick. "but I'm quite sure you'll find out."

Scarlett Fever

I

It was one those crisp, autumn-tinged November mornings that central Texans rarely get. The heat often begins in April—simmers—builds to a boil in August and barely slackens until December. With the heat people snarl, cursing the weather or each other. Some folks go limp with exhaustion or shoot someone to relieve the pressure cooker. But when the jet stream pushes cool Canadian air down across the plains and deep into the heart of Texas, people actually smile at each other and say inane things like "Isn't this weather great?" and "Reckon we might have some winter after all."

The old Balcones Fault line runs through the center of Austin, dividing the city east and west. The eastern side slopes to gently rolling hills. The western side is rougher terrain, full of limestone cliffs and hills and canyons. My office, on the fourth floor of the LaGrange Building, is in northwest Austin, and the building sits on a small hill. My apartment is only a few blocks from the LaGrange.

It was seven fifty-eight a.m. when I arrived. My partner, Cinnamon Jemima Gunn, or C.J., as she is known to most folks, is always in the office by eight a.m. We had just completed a big insurance fraud investigation and were behind on our paperwork, and I had promised to come in early. Okay, so eight is not exactly early to those who get up with the chickens, but it was early for me. I don't do single digits of the day well.

The telephone rang as I walked in, and C.J. answered. "G. & G. Investigations," she said, listening briefly. "Yes, Mr. Porter, Ms. Gordon just walked in. Will you hold a moment?" Her professional-signal tone clashed with the surprised roll of her eyes when she noted the early hour.

C.J. punched a button, held the receiver out, and with a wry expression said, "Bulldog Porter wants you, Jenny."

"Bulldog" King Porter, one of the best criminal defense attorneys money can buy, had sent work our way before. It began with us doing a bang-up job on the Loudermilk case, making Bulldog happy and a nice piece of change for us. His nickname came from being tenacious in court.

"You talk to him."

"I don't have time. He gets off on 'those old rum-running days in Galveston,' and ties a person up for hours."

Bulldog's stories can be endless, depending on his mood. I hurried into the inner office, not wanting to leave him dangling. "Mr. Porter, how are you?"

His voice held a chuckle. "I thought we'd gotten past that Mr. Porter and Mrs. Gordon stuff by now, Jenny."

"Well, we have, Bulldog, but . . ."

"Young lady, you don't have to be polite to an old curmudgeon. Can't say I deserve politeness even from a pretty lady like you."

I could picture him, the widow's peak and the thick steel-gray hair, his piercing blue eyes startling in his seventy-eight-year old face. I swiveled my chair around and looked out the window. A northerly wind swirled leaves around like a giant cake mixer whipping batter. Thick white clouds with black-streaked bottoms looked as if they would develop into thunder-boomers soon. "I'm sure you didn't call just to pass out compliments, Bulldog."

"Quite right. Complimenting you is a pleasant chore,

but I will get to the point. There's a young man I'd like you to see."

"Fine. One of your clients?"

"Not exactly. He's the son of an old and dear friend. The boy's about your age. His is an unusual story I think you should hear. He's looking for a young woman who's disappeared. Someone special, but he . . . well, perhaps he should tell you himself. He does, however, need a good investigator, and you lovely damsels at G. & G. fit the bill." Bulldog held a whispered conversation on his end and when he came back asked, "Are either you or C.J. available today? Perhaps right after lunch?"

"Yes, I believe so," I said, knowing full well we had all day free. "How does one o'clock sound?"

"One is fine. Wilson Billeau is my young friend's name. Thank you, Jenny, this means a lot. Wilson's like the son I never had. His father, Jud Billeau, and I were deputy D.A.s back in the fifties and sixties and we . . ."

Damn Sam. I choked back a sigh. He could go on for another half hour, but for once I got lucky. Bulldog's secretary, Martha May, interrupted him, saying he had a long distance call on another line. "I'll finish this story one day, Jenny. You'll enjoy it. And listen, I appreciate this."

"Don't mention it, Bulldog."

After hanging up, I walked out to our kitchen/storage room, grabbed a mug of coffee, and went to fill C.J. in on the conversation with Bulldog.

"Who does Porter think we are, the frigging Bureau of the Missing?" C.J.'s haughty tone made it all sound distasteful. She slammed drawers, shoved things around on her desk, and said, "A missing person, huh? Sounds boring, too."

Hoo boy, she's in one of her moods, I thought. But despite her gripes, I knew she'd never want us to refuse a paying customer.

My partner was a Pittsburgh police officer for eight years before moving back to her native Texas. She stands six feet tall, is built a lot like Racquel Welch, and reminds me of Nichelle Nichols, the actress who played in Star Trek, except C.J.'s skin tone is darker. Her tongue can be as sharp as a surgeon's scalpel.

Good paying customers are her favorite kind. She's not money-hungry, but her favorites are the ones with cash. We operate on a slim margin and, because of her excellent business head, manage to stay afloat.

"And who's going to pay for this?"

"I assume Mr. Billeau is paying. Bulldog didn't exactly say. Who cares? As long as we get paid."

"You got that right. I've been going over the bank statement this morning."

"We're not overdrawn?"

"No, but damn these companies who run sixty days behind. Afraid we could be in deep do-do before then."

Bank statements are Greek to me, and I round everything off to the nearest dollar. C.J. knows her balance to the exact penny. I'd once offered to keep our office books, but she said not until our sun goes super-nova. She does the books, but it makes her cranky.

"Well, if the client's due at one, you can grab his check out of his hand and hot-foot it to the bank before it closes."

"Aww, shit. Somebody has to worry about money around here."

"I know, and you do it so well I don't like to deprive you."

"You just remember to get a retainer. We don't do freebies." The computer keyboard began clicking again. "Why don't you get back to your desk and finish your reports?"

"Yessum, Miz Gunn, whatebber you say, Miz Gunn."

"Smart Ass. You ain't the right color to talk the talk."

"Discrimination again. Boy, the things I have to put up with around here." A Post-It notepad hit the doorjamb as I went through it.

I was tempted to say, Yah-ha ya missed me, but instead, I stuck my head around the corner of the door. "Are you going to join me when our client arrives?"

"Afraid not, Jen. I've got too much to do. These invoices need to go in tonight's mail."

"You just don't want to listen to a tale of lost love."

"You got that right. I heard enough of those when I was a cop." C.J. came to the door to stand in front of me. "Besides, you're so much better at that than I. You get all full of empathy, and the client loves that shit."

"Okay, I'll wing it alone, but if you think you can cut out early . . ."

"You just call me when the action begins." Her laugh was evil. "That's what I crave, Girlfriend. The excitement."

"You are so bad." I went back to my expense reports, glad she'd lightened up a bit.

Mr. Billeau walked in on time and introduced himself. He probably wasn't thirty yet, but he had one of those faces that would look boyish for the next thirty years. His thick auburn hair was cut short, not quite a crew cut. He had a narrow waist and broad shoulders that looked like he wore football pads. His plaid western shirt was clean, and his stone-washed Levis and scuffed cowboy boots—the working-type, not the fancy dress ones—completed the picture. A burnt orange and white gimme cap with a U.T. Longhorn logo was tucked under his left arm.

"Mr. Billeau?" I held out my hand. He looked for a moment as if he wasn't sure what to do and then took it. His hand was limp, but I gave him a firm shake and almost laughed at his surprise. Some men get uncomfortable when shaking hands with a woman. "I'm Jenny Gordon," I said. "And this is my partner, C.J. Gunn."

C.J. gave him a brief nod and went back to her monitor. Damn her, I thought, she could be a little more cordial, but she winked as I led the way to the inner office.

"We can talk more comfortably in here." Once inside I indicated an upholstered customer chair for him and turned to walk behind my desk. I stopped. He had followed only to the doorway.

"Mrs. Gordon, I'm not sure about this."

I put on my most disarming smile. "Fine, but you've made an effort to come here. Let's discuss it. If you decide there's nothing I can do to help," I said, "you can be on your way. It won't hurt my feelings."

He stared at his feet. When he finally looked up, I could see he'd decided to give me a try. He walked to the chair. "Mrs. Gordon, if you can help, I'll be obliged."

He sat down and stared at his feet again. He looked like a kid in high school taking a history test and looking for answers he'd written on his shoe tops.

Maybe he found something because he suddenly began talking. "I'm a country boy, Mrs. Gordon." He raised his head. "Probably a little dumb, too."

I smiled reassuringly after telling him to call me Jenny.

" 'Bout all I'm good at is farming. My grandpa left me a little place out near Dripping Springs. Nothing much, but it's mine. I raise a few chickens—milk a few cows. I work hard all week and come Saturday night, I like to go into town, maybe have a few beers."

"Sounds normal to me."

He began twisting the gimme cap in his large hands. "There's this one place I like to go to—The Lucky Star Bar and Grill. You heard of it?"

I admitted I hadn't.

"They have these girls that dance."

"With the customers?"

"No, ma'am. I mean dance on stage. They take off their clothes, too." He blushed. "For several weeks . . . one girl. She was so lovely and I, uh, I sorta fell for her."

I nodded, not wanting to interrupt.

"Every man who came in—fell for her. I mean, this girl—pretty as a speckled pup—dancing in this joint. She made you feel special. Everybody stopped whatever they were doing just to watch Scarlett dance."

"Scarlett?"

"Yes, ma'am. Her name is Scarlett Fever."

I almost made a joke, but he was so doggone serious. "What happened?"

"It's driving me crazy. Ten days ago her name was gone from that big sign out front. I went in and asked the bartender. He said she was gone. I asked where. He said maybe Los Angeles or Las Vegas. He didn't know. He thought she'd moved on to a bigger city where she could make bigger money.

"Miss Jenny. I've gone to Dallas, Los Angeles, Las Vegas, Houston, even Nashville. I can't find a trace. And ma'am, I've got to find her. She and I . . . Oh, we never went out or nothing, but I knew from the way she looked at me—we were meant to be."

Could anyone be so incredibly naive? He was such a country bumpkin. "Wilson, this world is full of big cities. Bigger and better places than Austin, Texas. She could be in any city."

"Yes, ma'am, I know it's hopeless. I might be dumb, but I'm not stupid." He blushed again. "It was crazy to come here. Take up your time." He studied his feet again for a moment. "But the crazy part. I'm afraid something bad has happened. I'll never believe she left without saying goodbye. And I don't know where else to turn. Mr. Porter said if anyone could find Scarlett, you could."

"His vote of confidence is nice, even if it is somewhat skewed."

Forlorn couldn't even begin to cover his hang-dog expression as he realized what I was implying. That I probably wouldn't be able to find her either.

C.J. had nailed it when she said clients love it when they feel you care. The police don't have time to give them personal attention. That's why they come to a private eye in the first place, but that's also why it hurts when you can't help.

Girls like Scarlett change locations about as often as the weather changes in central Texas, and they never leave a forwarding address. I knew what the odds were. An impossible mission, right?

No one was more surprised than I when the next words came out of my mouth. "Wilson, it's not hopeless." Did I really say that? "There are a couple of things I can do that might produce a lead."

"Like what?"

Yeah, like what, smart ass. Me and my big mouth. "First, I'd check where she worked. Maybe someone there knows something."

"Jim, the bartender, didn't know anything."

"Maybe she had a girlfriend and confided in her. What about the other dancers and the waitresses and the musicians?"

"I've already asked. Nobody knows nothing."

"Maybe they were leery about why you wanted to know. People working around singers and dancers, especially pretty ones, learn they have to be careful about giving out information. You can never tell who might be a sicko or a pervert. They might talk to me." A faint hope shined in his eyes. And strangely enough, I started having a little hope myself.

There were a few other places I could check—the owner of the club—the person who wrote the checks. Maybe a talent agency or a dancer's union. Surely a young woman moving on to greener pastures didn't do it entirely on her own. Someone, somewhere knew Scarlett and knew where she had gone.

"Wilson, why don't you give me a couple of days, let me see what I can turn up. That way you'll at least have the satisfaction of knowing you gave it your best shot."

"I'll be happy to pay whatever it cost. I've got money saved. A lot of money."

I almost said we could talk money later, but C.J. would have killed me. "Okay. A three hundred dollar retainer to begin. That's two days. We can settle expenses afterwards." I pulled a standard contract out of the top drawer of my desk.

He took out his billfold and handed me six fifty-dollar bills. "I feel better already. Just knowing someone will be doing something. I haven't been able to eat or sleep."

Wilson Billeau walked out feeling hopeful, and I wondered if I had lost my cotton-picking mind.

II

C.J. and I went into our missing persons routine. She began a paper chase via computer. Since legwork is my specialty, I drove out to the Lucky Star Bar and Grill.

Beginning in front of the State Capitol Building and driving south on South Congress Avenue, you pass through the downtown area, cross Town Lake and continue along where eventually the area becomes a strip of nightclubs, bars, motels and prowling grounds for pimps and prostitutes. A scuzzy area only a few short miles from the state's political power.

The club was on South Congress, a mile or so west of Interstate 35. As suspected, it had a western motif, a big white Lone Star on the roof and country music twanged inside; also, as suspected, no one thought it was unusual that Scarlett had left. Dancers work here and there—leaving when the mood struck.

Oh, she had mentioned moving on, but who knew which bright lights had lured her. One day she just ups and didn't show.

Jim, the bartender, looked like a Mexican bandito, but was talkative, except he didn't have a clue about Scarlett. I thanked him for his time and asked if he had a photograph of the girl. He found a black and white 8 x 10 publicity shot that the club had put in the lobby for promotion.

At the front door I had to pause to allow a young woman carrying a guitar case to come in, and Jim called out to me. "Hey, Detective Lady, this here's one of Scarlett's friends. I'll bet Delia Rose can tell you what you want to know."

The young woman was short, around twenty, a few pounds overweight, but chunky, not fat. Her straight blonde hair was pulled back into a pony tail. Her blue eyes, more knowing than they should be at her age, told of all the hard knocks she'd received in her short life.

The bartender introduced us, and Delia Rose and I slid into an empty booth. I told her I was a private investigator.

"And you've been hired to find Scarlett?"

I nodded.

"I'm sorry," she said. "Scarlett talked about going to Vegas, but I don't know if that's where she went. She didn't even tell me good-bye. I'm a little hurt, too, because I thought we were friends."

"Maybe she left with a boyfriend," I said. "Was there a special guy? Someone you remember coming in to see her?"

She began shaking her head before I was through talking.

"Look," I said. "She was a beautiful girl. Surely there was someone . . ."

"Not really. She flirted with everyone, but I don't think there was a boyfriend."

"Or a girlfriend?"

Delia Rose blushed. "She didn't have any designs that way either, and believe me I would have known."

"Who of the regulars did she pay attention to?"

She thought a moment. "Only one guy—a farm boy. Sweet kid. He had a funny name."

"Wilson Billeau?"

"Yeah, that was it. Wilson Billeau. He had the fever for Scarlett Fever." She realized her joke, and we laughed.

"He's my client."

"Scarlett was nice to his face, but she made fun of him behind his back." Delia Rose looked wistful. "Man, I wish someone would get that kind of hots for me."

I stood. "Well, I appreciate your help. If you think of anything, will you call?" I gave her my card.

Delia Rose arched an eyebrow and smiled. "When you find her, tell her I said to drop dead, okay?" She smiled wistfully again, and that's when I knew she also had the fever for Scarlett.

"Will do," I said.

Before I was halfway to the door, she called me back.

"I just thought of something. The day before Scarlett left, an older man came in. She was dancing and suddenly got a sick look. When she came offstage he grabbed her arm and said, 'We have to talk.' Scarlett pulled away and told him to leave her alone. His face got all red, and Scarlett had this funny look. Not scared exactly, but sorta like resigned.

"The old guy doubled up his fist, and I thought sure he was going to hit her. Jim saw the guy was acting up and came over. Told him we didn't want any trouble and asked him to leave."

"Did you ask her about this guy afterwards?"

"Yeah, but she said she didn't want to talk about him and for me to forget it. So I did. I guess I forgot all about it until just now."

"What did he look like?"

"Let's see, I can't remember much. Maybe late fifties. Dark hair, turning gray. Jim might remember. He got a better look."

She called Jim over, but he couldn't add much more. He said the guy was plain vanilla. "Some old fart. Dressed in a business suit that went out of style twenty years ago."

"I remember thinking at the time he reminded me of a movie star," said Delia Rose. "One of those older guys, but I can't remember who."

They couldn't think of anything else, and this time I really did leave.

I tacked Scarlett's picture to the wall next to my desk hoping to be inspired. A striking dark-haired woman, twenty-two or thereabouts. Her eyes were dark too, but with only a black and white photo, I couldn't be sure of exact colors. A smile extended to her come-hither eyes, yet there was an innocence, too. Try as I might, I couldn't see much to make her star-quality. Dark-haired beauties aren't exactly a novelty. Obviously, you had to have seen her dance moves.

Strippers don't belong to a union, but C.J. traced the photographer who'd taken the publicity picture. I talked to him and to the talent agency who'd booked Scarlett into the Lucky Star. Sure they knew her, but she hadn't confided any plans to them.

C.J.'s nimble computer fingers found no records of credit cards or bank accounts. Scarlett Fever didn't have a car registration or a driver's license, either, but C.J. discovered Scarlett had a room, for the past six months, at the Stagecoach Motel, a half-mile south of the Lucky Star. She was registered as Scarlett Fever O'Hara.

A trip to the motel seemed logical. It was sleazy-looking, more like a place for rent-by-the-hour trysts than a home for a young girl. The manager was also a sleaze-bag, but he took my twenty dollar bill greedily and gave me the key. The room was pathetic; an old iron bedstead held a sagging mattress, a vanity-type dresser from the fifties stood against one wall. Worn carpet and torn drapes over yellowed window shades completed the decor. I found a rust-speckled can of Lady Schick shave cream and one lipstick tube, fire engine red, used down to the metal. Nothing else to show a young woman had lived in that depressing room for six months—no clothes, no receipts, no pictures. Scarlett appeared and disappeared—end of story.

As I left I asked the manager how Scarlet got around as she didn't have a car. "How should I know? Walked maybe?"

My twenty must not have extended to his answering questions.

It was discouraging, although I hadn't expected much to begin with. Yet one tiny cell in the back of my brain kept taunting in a sing-song voice, "Nah-na, nah-na, nah-na—you've forgotten something."

C.J. and I checked and double-checked every scrap of information we had. It was wasted time.

At the end of two days I called Wilson Billeau. He didn't seem surprised. The slight hope he'd nursed must have dwindled soon after he'd left our office.

"Thanks for trying, ma'am. I know you did your best."

"Wilson, I believe things happen for a reason. Scarlett came into your life. Maybe to remind you that you ought to do something besides muck around with cows and chickens. I'll bet if you tried, you'd find a young lady who'd like to live on a farm in Dripping Springs."

"I guess. I promised myself I'd put this all behind me if you couldn't find her, but I can't give up yet." His voice didn't sound as if his heart was in it, but he was determined.

I wished him luck and broke the connection.

C.J. said Wilson's money helped to ease our cash flow, but the whole episode left me feeling sad for a couple of days. Soon though, we both put the missing Scarlett Fever out of our minds.

III

Three weeks later, I unfolded the morning newspaper, *The Austin American Statesman* and, there she was—Scarlett Fever O'Hara. The grainy picture was the same publicity photo I had, and she was identified only as Scarlett. The headline for this rainy December day read SCARLETT IS

DEAD. The story said a hooker's nude body had been found in one of Austin's better downtown hotel rooms. The woman had been beaten severely and then stabbed to death.

Unholy murder served up with notes of Christmas cheer.

A man registered to that room as Marshall Tolliver from Houston was now in police custody.

C.J. called me at home. "Did you see her?"

We discussed the murder for a few minutes, and I said I'd better contact Wilson Billeau. "I hope he's already seen the paper because I'd hate to be the one to tell him."

There was no answer when I called Wilson, so I tried Bulldog Porter. The attorney said one of his informants had called him soon after the girl's body was found, and he'd notified Wilson of the girl's death. He said Wilson had gone to the funeral home to make arrangements for her and would drop by Bulldog's office later. Bulldog said he would give Wilson our condolences.

My next call was to Lieutenant Larry Hays. Larry works in the homicide unit of the Austin Police Department. He and I have been good friends for years. I'd first met him when he and my late husband, Tommy Gordon, entered the police academy together. They were partners until Tommy left APD to become a private detective.

After Tommy's death Larry took a brotherly role with me. One I was grateful for, except when he got too protective. Especially where it related to the detective agency. Larry is sensitive, witty, and stubborn as only a Swede can be. He is also one hell of a good cop.

When he returned my call, I asked, "What's the story on the dead hooker?"

"The one known as Scarlett? What do you know about it?"

"Nothing about the murder, but . . ."

"Just a minute." Larry put me on hold, briefly. When he came back, he said in his official voice, "Meet me at Casa Mañana!"

His gruff, insistent order hit me the way that tone usually does, and I almost told him to go take a flying leap from the Congress Avenue bridge, but with a conciliatory tone he said, "Please, Jenny. I could use your help here."

I said I'd be there by one-thirty.

Casa Mañana is a Tex-Mex restaurant near APD headquarters, and the officers frequently go there for lunch. It's a converted old stucco house, yellow with green trim and the feel of a cantina. Inside were plain wooden tables covered with oilcloth, and the tables at each booth had Mexican tile tops. The food was excellent, the price reasonable and the service topnotch.

Larry is attractive, long-legged, and wears a size 13 shoe. He's five years older than me, and I was unmerciful when he turned forty recently. He was seated in the corner booth when I arrived, two iced teas, hot salsa and tortilla chips already on the table. I slid into the booth and he said, "Where you been keeping yourself?"

"C.J.'s been cracking the whip. We've hardly had time to go to the bathroom."

"That explains your pained expression."

"If I have a pained expression, it's because you haven't called or come by to see us."

"Hah! I used to complain when we had one homicide a month. Little did I know those were the good old days."

"Makes you wonder what's happening to our normally laid-back capital city."

"Fast growth, drugs and hard times."

We were interrupted by Paco Hidalgo, the owner, as he placed chicken enchiladas—with all the trimmings—on the table and refilled my glass. The chips and salsa I'd been nibbling called for constant mouth-cooling, but I get anemic if I don't get my quota of Mexican food.

"I hope you don't mind, but I ordered your usual. Thought we could save time." Larry began eating without waiting for my reply. "Tell me what you know about Scarlett."

I filled him in on Wilson Billeau and the saga of Scarlett, and on everything C.J. and I had done. "Everyone I talked to was convinced she'd left for more bucks and glory elsewhere." It was difficult trying to talk and eat too, but I managed. "What's the story on this guy you've arrested?"

"Tolliver tells a straightforward tale with only one twist. Says he was in town for a sales conference and he picked her up yesterday afternoon at the hotel bar." Larry was shoveling his food and didn't let the talk slow him down. "They spent a short time talking and indulged in a little slap and tickle. He figured she was a hooker, working the convention, but he didn't mind."

"Does he have a record?"

"Nope. He's squeaky clean."

"Then what's the twist?"

"Somebody slipped him a Mickey Finn," he said. "We had a few last year. Hookers setting up and rolling out-of-towners. First one I've seen this year though."

"But why did he kill her?"

"The captain thinks Tolliver woke up earlier than expected. Caught the woman with her hand in his billfold and flew into a rage." Larry finished his food and Paco unobtrusively removed the plate.

"You don't agree?"

"I don't know. Maybe I've got a burr up my tail. I think his story about waking up at one o'clock this morning and finding her dead in his bathroom is the truth."

I shuddered. Finding a woman in the bathroom stabbed to death gave me the willies.

"It won't be easy to prove his innocence. He claims he never saw the knife before, but it was there in the shower, his prints on it. Two points in his favor is that he didn't run. He called the cops and waited until they showed. His hands were also unmarked."

"Why wouldn't he hide the knife?"

"Exactly. Or wipe his prints. Tolliver says he picked it up without thinking." Larry lit up one of his favored cigarillos. "He wasn't too coherent during questioning; he acted much like a person would if they'd been given a Mickey."

"Do you have a better ID for the girl than Scarlett Fever O'Hara?"

Larry nearly choked on his iced tea. "Are you shitting me? Scarlett Fever O'Hara?"

"She danced at the Lucky Star Bar and Grill as Scarlett Fever. But she was registered at the Stagecoach Motel under Scarlett Fever O'Hara."

"The Stagecoach Motel, huh? We don't have that yet. Where is it?"

"On South Congress just before you get to 71."

"I'd better make a trip out there. They took her prints at the morgue and are running a search with AFIS (Automated Fingerprint Identification System.) If she's been arrested, we'll get a positive ID and her real name."

"She'd moved out; the place was empty. It's probably been rented to someone else by now." When I saw his face, I knew I'd said too much. "How could I know it was going to be a murder investigation? That was three weeks ago."

Larry tried, but couldn't hold his serious face and

smiled. "You bribed the clerk?"

"Let's say I donated to his favorite charity."

"I'll still need to talk to him—the sooner the better." He punched his cigarillo out in the ashtray, stood up and grabbed his wallet. "Thanks for the info, Jen."

"Thanks for lunch. You *are* buying?" I walked with him to the cash register.

"Sure. You saved me some leg work. That's worth lunch."

"Christmas will be here soon," I said, as we walked into the bright sunshine.

"And someone's daughter won't be home. God, I hate this time of year." He walked with me to my car. "That photo didn't do her justice," he said, as he bent to give me a brotherly good-bye kiss.

I headed for the Interstate wanting to get back to work before I started thinking about Wilson Billeau and his beautiful dead Scarlett and got depressed.

IV

Damn Sam. I was northbound, four miles from my exit, when it hit me, that niggling little thing I'd overlooked earlier. Dancers work out all the time; they have to to stay in shape. Why not strippers? Especially one hoping to latch on to a star. Neither C.J. nor I had thought about checking for a dance studio or health spa. I found a clear space in traffic, wrenched my car across the lanes, squealed off at the exit, crossed under the underpass, and headed down the southbound entrance ramp. Once I was going in the right direction, I picked up the Cellular phone and dialed. "C.J.? What dance studios or panting palaces are near The Lucky

Star or the Stagecoach Motel?"

"What do you think I am? The frigging information op . . ." She caught on fast. "Scarlett, huh?"

"You got that right. Why didn't we . . . ?"

"It was slim to none. She wasn't into ballet."

"Yeah, but." I couldn't explain the feeling, some inner instinct. "It's a long shot."

"I've gone out on a lot less before, Girlfriend." She gave me names and addresses of two dance places and three health clubs in the area. "Let me know what you find out."

The dance studios were a bust, ditto the first health club. The next sweat box on the list didn't sound promising because of its name, but nothing ventured and all that.

The Texas Gym and Health Spa was three miles south of the Lucky Star. For boxer and weight-lifter types only, I thought. A dirty beige concrete block building, it looked like it went out of business in 1969. A sign in the front window said OPEN. I walked in and the stale odor of sweat almost made me walk back out again. The reception area was small, a motel-style counter and doors on each side leading to open hallways. LADY'S GYM right and MEN'S GYM left. So it was coed. A door behind the counter led to what probably was an office.

A man of indeterminate age came out from the MEN'S side. He had on sweat pants and a form-fitting T-shirt which didn't do a thing for the extra fifty pounds he carried in his belly. His arms and shoulders were huge, but his face drew your attention. A deep red scar began at his nose and curled down across his chin. His small eyes were buried in folds of fat. How could he convince anyone they needed to shape up?

"Are you the manager?"

"The manager ain't here now. I'm his helper." He spoke

slowly, like he had to think about what I said and then think about what he was going to say before he said it.

"When do you expect him?"

"Tonight. He's got a funeral this afternoon."

That one threw me. "What?"

The man guffawed. "That's right, Brother Adkins owns this gym and he's a preacher, too." He scratched his chin along the edge of the scar. "Brother Adkins says the body is a Holy Temple and we should treat it as such."

A strange combination, if you ask me, but perhaps it did make a sort of weird sense. "Guess I never thought of it that way."

"Can I show you around?"

"No, I really needed to talk to . . ."

"I'm Buddy. He leaves me in charge when he's gone. I'm sure I can help you."

Taking the photo out of my purse, I said, "I'm Jenny Gordon, a private detective. I'm trying to find this young woman." I held the picture out. He took it and studied it as if memorizing some state secret.

Eventually he looked up and said, "She sure looks like Miss Henrietta, but it can't be. This girl is older and too painted up."

"Miss Henrietta?"

"She's Brother Adkins' daughter." He looked at the picture again. "I'm sure it's not her."

"Where would I find Miss Henrietta?"

"She's gone. Brother Adkins said something about her going up to Dallas a few days ago. I don't think she's come back yet."

This was maybe even a longer shot now, but I'd already started down this path and hated to give up. "And you're sure this isn't Henrietta Adkins?"

164

Buddy looked again. "No, it's not Miss Henrietta, but it looks like her older sister."

"Does Miss Adkins have an older sister?"

"I don't think so. Brother Adkins never told it to me. Henrietta never said nothing about a sister either." Buddy stared at me, his gaze almost as intent as the one he'd given the photo. "Did you say you was a cop?"

"No. I didn't say that, Buddy. I'm a private detective. Looking for this missing girl."

"Oh, yeah. You said that when you come in."

"I'd like to talk to the Reverend. Maybe he saw this girl. Someone said she used to work out here."

"I didn't never see her." He looked at his watch. "He'll have go to the cemetery for the graveside."

"Will he come back here after the cemetery?"

"Maybe. In an hour . . . I guess."

"Thanks, I'll come back in an hour." I stopped at the door and asked, "Is Miss Henrietta a dancer—like a ballet dancer?"

"No way. Dancing is forbidden by the Word. It's a sin and ab-bomi-nee-tion for a woman to call attention to herself." He stumbled over the four-syllable word.

"I understand. Well, thanks. Don't work out too hard; you don't want to strain a muscle." He gave me a puzzled look as I left. It taxed his brain too much to figure that one.

A hamburger emporium was a block down and across from the gym. I went inside, ordered a large iced tea, and found a pay phone.

"C.J.?" I told her about Brother Adkins and his daughter. "Can you check family records to see if there's another child, an older girl?"

"Like a black sheep daughter?"

"Maybe. Something's there, but I don't know what or how it connects."

"No problemo." Our other phone line rang. "Check you later, Girlfriend. Bye."

I sat in a booth facing the gym and sipped on my drink. I took out a pocket notebook and tried to make sense out of what I knew and what I didn't. Mostly, I doodled.

All the tea I'd had for lunch added to these extra ounces soon sent me scurrying to the LADIES. I hated to leave my looking post, but when you gotta go . . .

A maroon station wagon, a sign on the side reading Texas Gym & Health Spa, had pulled up while I was answering nature's call, and I saw a slender man in a dark leisure suit walking up to the gym's entrance. That must be Preacher Adkins, I thought, hustling out and hurrying across the street.

The reception area was empty. I crossed behind the counter and stuck my head into the office. The man I assumed to be Adkins was bent over the open drawer of a file cabinet.

I knocked on the doorjamb.

He whirled around. "Who are y..you?" His gray eyes in his narrow oval face showed surprise. He was about six feet tall, his muscular arms and legs well defined under the suit. A product of his own sound-body-dictum, probably. He had graying hair, thin, disapproving lips and a deep cleft in his chin. It was the Kirk Douglas dimple that fit Delia Rose's description of an older movie star.

"Sorry. I didn't mean to startle you, Brother Adkins. I'm Jenny Gordon. I'm trying to locate a missing girl who supposedly worked out here. I'm hoping you might know her." I noticed the faint indentation in Scarlett's chin on the photo I handed to him. Hard to deny family genes, I thought.

He took the photograph and glanced at it briefly. "I don't know her. She may have been in here, but I don't think so."

"Are you sure? I was told this girl resembles your daughter?"

"You've been talking to Buddy," he said, handing the picture back. "You can't pay too much attention to him. His brain is addled from taking too many jabs to the head. Every photograph he sees of a girl looks like Henrietta to him. He has a big crush on her."

"Then this girl doesn't look like your daughter?"

"No." He evaded my eyes and his voice grew indignant. "My daughter is younger, more beautiful and innocent. She has blue eyes and blonde hair. Henrietta would never paint herself up like a harlot either."

"Is Henrietta your only daughter?"

"My only child. My wife died in childbirth."

The part about his wife was true maybe, but I didn't believe for a minute he only had one child. "I'm sorry."

"It was a long time ago. I'm sure The Lord had a greater need for her than we did."

"This young woman is lying stone-cold in the Travis County morgue. Unloved and unwanted," I said, hoping for some reaction. "Somebody's family will miss her this Christmas."

His voice took on the timbre of the hellfire and brimstone evangelist. "I read about this harlot in the newspaper. She was a sinner, a whore. She doesn't deserve a Christian burial."

"That's one way of looking at it," I said. "Whatever happened to Christian forgiveness?"

"The Lord Almighty is the only One who can forgive sins. He will finally turn away from you if you keep rejecting him, just like some parents have to turn away from their children."

He'd justified it all in his mind, and I didn't have any argument for that. "Thanks for your time," I said, anxious to get away from this holier-than-thou Bible-thumper. No wonder Scarlett wanted to be anonymous. Henrietta probably felt the same way. "I'd like to call Henrietta . . ."

He pointed a finger at me and shouted, "Get out of here, you Jezebel. And you stay away from Henrietta. She has nothing to do with harlots and whores."

I'd never been accused of being a Jezebel before. It was time to go before he started throwing stones at me.

V

Information poured from the office printer like hail coming from a Texas tornado cloud, amazing my technological aptitude of a horned toad with its speed. C.J. got all the information we needed without ever leaving her desk.

Two legal document copies blew away all my theories. Texas birth certificates require a response to: other children born to this mother? And more specifically: how many other children are now living? Henrietta Jo Adkins was the only child born to Mary Madeline Fever Adkins. A death certificate for the wife of Stephen Adkins showed Madeline died on January 29, 1970, from heart failure. "Fever" wasn't just part of Scarlett's clever stage name; it was also her mother's maiden name. I'd been so sure there was an older daughter, but Henrietta Adkins and Scarlett Fever O'Hara had to be one and the same.

"Any other proof?" I asked C.J.

"Uh-huh. Scarlett was arrested for solicitation twice

under the name of Henrietta Jo Adkins. The Austin police department AFIS computer matched their fingerprints."

Preacher Adkins' attitude still infuriated me. "That sanctimonious bastard doesn't even intend to bury his own flesh and blood. Doesn't he care or know that Wilson is claiming the body?"

"No, because the heartless S.O.B. disowned her completely. But I hope he feels some fear right about now."

"Because his daughter was identified as a hooker?"

"You got it," said C.J. "His little church flock will probably tar and feather him. His reputation is ruined and . . ."

"Maybe he killed her to keep his reputation intact."

"Good thinking, Jenny."

"We seem to have a plethora of male suspects," I said.

"Marshall Tolliver, the man found in the room with the very dead Scarlett, and Preacher Adkins. Who else?"

"Buddy, the pug-ugly down at the gym. Except I can't see him being smart enough to carry out the complications of Mickey Finns. And . . . Wilson Billeau."

"Surely you don't think our good old country boy killed the girl he claims to love? Besides he's our client."

"He's technically not ours anymore. It's happened before, even to us." I knew she didn't want to be reminded about when her cousin, Veronica, and Veronica's baby had been killed, so I continued. "If we rule out Buddy, we still have three viable suspects. You do know it's not exactly our business to get into an active homicide case."

"Larry Hays would never forgive us."

"Understatement of the year. Yet you and I know what a heavy case load he has. He won't devote much time trying to solve a hooker's murder."

"What have you got in mind?"

"Not a darn thing, but if we put our heads together, we

169

should be able to come up with someone who might have wanted Scarlett dead."

"Exactly, and who was around to do it."

We brainstormed for an hour and couldn't figure out how to bypass Larry without causing trouble. "Maybe we should lay low and see what happens."

"I'd much rather stir things up and see what happens," said C.J. with an evil grin.

"What do we do about Mr. Tolliver?" I asked.

"After what Larry told you earlier," she said, "we can probably rule him out. If we talk to the hotel employees we might collaborate his story."

"Larry's team has already done that, I would imagine."

"Okay, let's head out to Dripping Springs to see what Wilson Billeau has to say and come back by the Lucky Star. We can stop in there for a cold beer. Talk to some folks."

C.J. drove us to Wilson's house with the top down on her Mustang. It was a great evening for a drive, but I didn't feel much like talking. I kept thinking how Wilson was really a sweet kid and how it would upset me if he was involved. C.J. knew how I felt, or maybe she even felt the same way, because she kept quiet too.

Bulldog Porter's Lincoln Towncar was in the driveway, and he greeted us at the door, a finger to his lips. "Wilson is lying down. He could use some feminine company. I'm not too good at this."

We walked into the living room and sat down. "The police called my office a short time ago," said Bulldog. "They knew I represented the man who claimed Scarlett's body and made the funeral arrangements. They said she'd been identified as Henrietta Adkins, but I can only say the name Wilson always used."

Wilson had heard us come in, and he joined us. "Do you

know if the police have arrested the man who killed her yet?" he asked without preamble. "Bulldog said they cleared that man from Houston, and he was released from jail." His face showed the ravages of grief, and his eyes were red-rimmed. He was suffering. If it was an act, it was the Oscar-winning performance of the year.

C.J. and I looked at each other. An unspoken message passed between us. This young man can't be the killer.

"We haven't talked to the police in the past few hours," I said. "I think our friend in homicide will call when APD makes an arrest."

Wilson said Scarlett's father still wanted no part of claiming her, so the funeral would be as he'd planned, to-morrow at two p.m. He said he hoped we'd come. We said we'd be there, and he went back to the bedroom.

I could tell Bulldog was grieving along with Wilson. He ob-viously had unusually strong feelings about his friend's son.

Bulldog said, "I've told Wilson the police will do their best, but they'll soon give up unless the killer drops in their lap. They don't have the time to devote to a long investiga-tion. Wilson would like you to take the case when the police give up."

We finally agreed to do what we legally could.

Bulldog was nodding off as we left, but Wilson came out to walk to the car with us. "Jenny, would you and C.J. promise me one thing?" he asked. For the first time since we arrived, his voice had some emotion. "No matter how long it takes or how much it costs, I want you to keep on looking. I want whoever killed her to rot in jail."

"We'll do our best," I said. "But as far as the jail term, Wilson, you know today's justice system—the killer may only serve a short time or get off completely. It's up to a judge and jury."

C.J. and I headed back to Austin.

"I can't help feeling sorry for him," I said. "For someone who'd never dated that girl, much less had a relationship with her, he's in bad shape. Did you see those big sad eyes?"

"She represented a fantasy to him, a dream," said C.J. "A dream that died. That's what had been worrying me. I was afraid he might have been too obsessed. That when he'd found out she was a hooker he didn't want anyone else to touch her."

"I know. Deep down I was afraid of the same thing. Are you confident he's innocent?"

"Yes. And if Larry has cleared Marshall Tolliver—that poor sucker from Houston—there's only one suspect left."

"Scarlett's unforgiving father," I said.

"And if Larry's as smart as I think he is, he's already checking Adkins from top to bottom. Let's go to the Hyatt for some fajitas," she said. "We can eat and talk about our options."

"I can't do it. I had a humongous lunch. We could go over to my house, and I'll fix a salad and grill a steak or a chicken breast for you."

C.J. is a big gal and eats like a construction worker. Luckily she never gains an ounce, but she also lifts weights, swims, and does martial arts training.

When we reached my apartment C.J. parked and opened her car door. "I hope you have a cold beer—I could use one, maybe even two."

We went inside. I went to the kitchen and got out a couple of Lite Coors. "I'll make up the bed in the guest room for you, and we won't worry about you driving home tonight."

"That works for me," C.J. said and popped the top on her can.

I popped mine also and checked for my telephone messages. One was a hang-up, and the other was Bulldog Porter. "Jenny? Are you there? Wilson has talked himself into doing something drastic. He's on his way now to talk to Scarlett's father. He thinks Adkins had something to do with killing her. I dozed off, but he left me a note. Wait, I've got Adkins's home address here."

Papers rustled noisily, then Bulldog gave out the preacher's address. "That's just off William Cannon and West Gate. We've got to stop him. I'm heading over there now." A moment later Bulldog said, "It's 9:05."

"Holy Shit! That was over forty minutes ago," said C.J. "Let's go."

The barely-sipped beer went down the drain and we left. The address where Preacher Adkins lived was five or six miles farther south and two or three miles west of the Lucky Star Bar and Grill It was a yuppified suburban area a good thirty to forty minutes from my apartment even at this time of night and using the freeway.

"MiGod, C.J. Did you see this coming?"

"No way. But in hindsight, I should have. Wilson was a man in pain, and he wants a killer brought to justice."

"And I just had to remind him justice was blind and deaf."

"He didn't need you to figure that out, Girlfriend."

"I know, but damn. Damn, damn."

As we raced down Interstate-35 I called Larry's house and office. No answer at either place. I dialed his pager and punched in our number. He still had not responded when we exited on William Cannon Drive and turned into a subdivision. The houses along here were a little older than others in the upscale section down the block. When we neared the address, I spotted Larry's car parked behind two patrol units, their red and blue lights stabbing the darkness.

A Special Missions Team (SMT) was there, tall men dressed in black, with helmets and equipment hanging from everywhere. They carried heavy firepower and looked like alien warriors from Star Wars.

Two uniformed patrolmen kept back a small knot of thrill-seekers and, as we parked, I saw the SMT squad move out surrounding the house.

Bulldog's Lincoln Towncar was angled up to the edge of the lawn two houses away. We parked on the opposite side of the street. When he saw us he opened his car door and waved us over. "Can you find out what's going on?" he asked. "No one will tell me anything."

"They haven't let you talk to Wilson?" I said. "Don't they know you might be able to talk some sense into him? Come on, we'll try to find someone in charge."

The three of us walked slowly toward the house, edging our way through people politely so the uniformed officers wouldn't think we were troublemakers. As we reached one of the patrolmen, a shot was fired, coming from inside the house.

A second shot followed, moments later. Both shots sounded like they were from the same handgun and not one of the rifles the SMT officers used.

"I don't think Wilson has a gun," said Bulldog.

The SMT squad swarmed in and someone yelled, "He's down."

I knew it would be awhile before we would know anything. Two ambulances squealed up, one behind the other, and the silence when they turned off the sirens was exquisite. The EMS attendants ran inside the house.

"That's a good sign, isn't it?" asked Bulldog. "Someone needs medical attention."

"It could mean anything, Bulldog," I said. "Don't get your hopes too high."

When the M.E.'s station wagon pulled up a few minutes later, I had to catch Bulldog when he slumped. I eased the old man to a sitting position on the ground and C.J., with tightened lips, said she was going to find Larry Hays and get some answers.

Time passed, and I couldn't get Bulldog to go to his car. We sat in the dewy grass, and I kept my arm around his shaking bony shoulders. Neither of us talked.

When C.J. returned to where we sat, one of the EMS attendants followed, and I could tell from her face the news was grim. "They're both . . ." She shook her head. "Looks like they fought. The preacher had a gun. After he shot Wilson, he killed himself."

Bulldog started having chest pains. "He—Wilson was my son," Bulldog said, breaking down. "His legal father was my best friend, but no one except his mother and I ever knew he was really my son."

Stunned, I watched the EMS guys begin checking the old man. Bulldog was Wilson's natural father? I couldn't believe it.

C.J. took me aside. "The police found news clippings of Adkins being convicted of child abuse. He'd beaten up on Scarlett for years. Larry Hays had already found out that Adkins had served time for that conviction in another state and had been released from prison six months ago. There was also a letter of resignation to his church in which he admitted killing his daughter. Claimed she was a seed of Satan and had to be destroyed."

The medics reported that Bulldog didn't have a heart attack; it was emotional stress. They put him on a stretcher saying a checkup at the hospital was routine procedure. I said I'd ride with him in the ambulance, and C.J. said she'd meet me there.

The EMS wagon was ready to roll, but I couldn't get in yet. "Naive little shit." The tears I'd held back slipped out. "What could we have done differently, C.J.? What more?"

"Nothing," she said, putting an arm around me. "Not a damn thing."

"Why? C.J., why?"

"The Scarlet Fever got hold of Wilson and never let go."

The author thanks Kenny Rogers for writing and recording the song "Scarlet Fever" which inspired this story.

Ruby Nell's Ordeal

I

Nurse's aide Vanita Gomez was tired when she walked into the employee lounge of the Adobe Creek Nursing Center at 10:25 p.m. on Friday night. She worked the graveyard shift four evenings a week, Thursdays through Sundays. She also worked Monday through Friday at the Adobe County Health Center from ten to four, which would explain her fatigue. As a single parent with two high schoolers, it took two jobs to stay afloat.

She only half-listened to Sonja Walker, R.N., the outgoing charge nurse. All incoming personnel were required to hear a verbal report on the status of each patient for the previous eight hours. Usually there were only a few changes; ninety percent of the patients were just being warehoused until they died, and they did all die. Some quickly and some slowly, inch by inch. Whenever possible, Vanita tried to be beside them when the end came.

Vanita thought it was sad for a person to live a vital productive life for seventy or eighty years, then end up this way. Pitiful little things, she thought, so helpless. Draining emotions and resources from their families. Why, she wondered, unable to stop herself from questioning, hadn't the Good Lord come up with a better plan for a human's departure? Something painless while the body was still mobile and the mind still alert.

In the meantime she wiped their behinds and forced the pureed food down their throats and turned their helpless bodies every two hours. She smoothed limp hair and lotioned dry withered limbs and sometimes cried silent tears as she worked. Some cursed her or reviled her for her efforts, but usually they were grateful for small comforts, comforts like getting their teeth brushed or their fingernails cut. Their gratitude would show in their eyes even when their words were nonsense.

Vanita took care of the patients on Two-West, Rooms 200 through 210; half were private rooms and the remainder semi-private. Full beds meant seventeen patients, but at night the patients mostly slept so it wasn't difficult. Besides Vanita, four other aides, an LVN charge nurse and one orderly made up the floor's night crew.

Sonja Walker, R.N., droned on—giving blood pressures, temperatures, pulse rates, medicine changes, orders from doctors, X-rays, and lab tests scheduled and completed. From the nurse's notes she told of special problems, like who wasn't eating well and who had sluggish bodily functions, about visits from family or friends and the other myriad of details for each hour of the eight she had been on duty.

Vanita was half-listening, half-dozing, when she noticed a flash of movement out of the corner of her eye. She turned and saw a woman dressed in a black coat walking rapidly down the corridor toward room 202.

Vanita was poised to go after the woman to inquire about the nature of this late visit when she realized it was Ruby Nell Poteet visiting her mother. Mrs. Poteet's prognosis wasn't good. She had pneumonia and was fading fast.

Vanita felt sorry for Ruby Nell. Mrs. Poteet was often as cranky as a long-tailed cat in a roomful of rocking chairs. Ruby Nell, as the only child, had practically given up her own life for her mother, but carried her burden without complaint.

Vanita settled back in her chair and noted Sonja Walker had finished the report. Sonja did have a final caution. "Keep an alert eye on Mr. Jenkins in room 206. He's got a wild hair about his wife, Maureen. Says she's been whoring around on him."

"But she's dead, isn't she?" asked Vanita.

"Two years now, but he doesn't remember. Twice today he got up all by himself and went stomping down the hall calling for Maureen at the top of his lungs. We had to get the orderlies from the first floor to help get him back in bed." Sonja closed the charts. "That's it, boys and girls," she said. "I'm out of this snake pit until Monday. Y'all have fun, now."

An hour later, Vanita Gomez walked to the nurse's station and informed Cynthia Washington, LVN, that Mrs. Poteet had expired. "Poor little soul can rest now," Vanita said.

II

When Sheriff Damon Dunlap came in for lunch he was unusually quiet. His wife, Robbie, could tell he was worried, but she didn't ask what was on his mind. She figured Damon was mulling it over. After nearly thirty years of marriage, she knew he'd tell her, sooner or later, using her as a sounding board for whatever he was worrying about.

Robbie liked hearing about his cases. Damon said she had a morbid curiosity about things criminal. She placed bowls of homemade beef stew on the table, and as they were sitting down, the front doorbell rang. It was Ruby Nell Poteet.

Ruby Nell was a twittery little woman approaching sixty.

She had hair dyed an orangey-red color that some women her age thought was becoming, but wasn't. "I'm sorry to disturb you, Robbie," she said. "But I have to talk to Damon. It's important."

Damon led Ruby Nell Poteet into his study, and Robbie put her husband's lunch in the icebox. Why did they always come by at lunch time? she wondered, shaking her head. The sheriff's office kept routine business hours, which was ignored about half the time. In small towns people felt the sheriff was their own personal law-keeper. They put him in office, and they could vote him out again.

Robbie Dunlap liked living in Frontier City, the county seat of Adobe County. She had grown up here and couldn't imagine living anywhere else. The town's population of a few thousand was nestled in the rugged limestone hill country, northwest of Austin. It was a pretty town, progressive, with a bunch of wonderful people and only a few troublemakers.

But because they lived six blocks from the courthouse square, Damon often received sheriffing visits at the most inopportune times. Robbie didn't begrudge them, but drop-ins upset her work schedule, and that aggravated her.

At fifty-five, and with their two children grown and fending for themselves, Robbie had decided to fulfill her dream of writing mysteries. She'd sold several short stories to the national magazines and recently submitted a partial manuscript: three chapters and a synopsis to the River City Mystery Association's First Novel Contest.

She'd already won the local and state contests in the P.I. subgenre category. The regionals were next, and her hopes of making it all the way to nationals were running high. The ultimate goal, winning the nationals, was an exciting challenge. The $15,000 first prize and publication of her book would help alleviate the guilt she had from giving up her job as an X-ray technician and give her ego a tremendous boost. Adobe County sheriff's pay wasn't the greatest, and that first prize check would give their finances a tremendous boost, too.

To be eligible for the regionals, Robbie's manuscript had to be completed. The first draft was almost done, and the deadline was coming up fast. Being interrupted put her behind in her afternoon writing schedule. She hated being put behind.

"Robbie," Damon called out. "Can you come in here a minute?"

His request was unexpected. People usually wanted these talks with Damon to be confidential. Robbie was curious as she wiped her hands on a dish towel and walked to the study.

Ruby Nell Potcet, sitting in the big lounge chair, was crying, while Damon stood near the window looking angry. "We've got ourselves a problem here," Damon said in a terse voice.

"What's wrong?"

"Ruby Nell's mother passed away around midnight last night," he answered.

"Oh, Ruby Nell." Robbie knelt quickly by the chair and patted the woman's arm. "I'm sorry. I hadn't heard." Robbie looked at Damon and signaled an unspoken "what's up?", but he shook his head. She noticed his tightened lips and stiff shoulders. Something was definitely wrong.

"Ohhh, Rob-bbi-ee." Ruby Nell sobbed. "Damon thinks I-I, uh, killed Mama."

Her husband seldom jumped to conclusions, and she was surprised by his lack of sympathy. "Damon Dunlap," said Robbie, standing and turning to him with astonishment. "I don't—"

"Wait just a minute, Ruby Nell," Damon interrupted. "I didn't accuse you of any such thing." When he spoke in his official voice he sounded as if all his six feet, four inches, two hundred thirty-eight pounds could smash you in a New York minute. And he could. But he never smashed women or even intimidated them. People usually relied on him when they were in pain or sorrow.

Ruby Nell began to caterwaul; she was on the edge of hysteria.

Robbie put her fists on her hips. "Damon, I don't care what the problem is. I won't have someone treated this way in my house. Go to the kitchen, please, and pour a glass of brandy for Ruby Nell." Robbie fought to control her temper.

Damon hesitated only a moment before he complied. He returned with the glass and handed it to Ruby Nell, who sputtered down half the contents.

Robbie walked down the hall to the bathroom, wet a wash cloth in cool water, came back and gave the cloth to the older woman.

In a few minutes, Ruby Nell seemed sufficiently calmed, and Damon's stance became that of a concerned friend again. "I'm sorry, Ruby Nell," he said. "I didn't mean to upset you."

"Tell me what's going on, Damon. I can't believe you suspect Ruby Nell of murder."

Damon sighed and used "The Sheriff" voice again. "This is an official investigation, and since Miss Poteet is potentially a suspect, we shouldn't discuss it informally like this."

"Has she been charged with anything?" asked Robbie. "Are you arresting her?"

"No, of course not."

"Then I don't see any problem."

Ruby Nell spoke up. "Mr. Schmidt over at Schmidt-Weizer Funeral Home wouldn't let me see Mama's body yet. When I asked why, he wouldn't say. I persisted. Finally, he admitted there were some unexplained bruises on her neck, and that it looked like someone had smothered her to death. He said he'd reported his findings to the Sheriff."

"I'm with you so far," said Robbie.

"I've been investigating all morning," said Damon. "I'm not at liberty to say what I've found. Naturally, I want to question Ruby Nell, but I think she should have a lawyer present when I do."

"Okay," said Robbie. "That's reasonable."

Ruby Nell said, "I came over to ask Damon what was going on about Mama, never dreaming he would think I killed her. Why would anyone kill Mama?"

"Ruby Nell," said Damon. "You'd better not say anything else without your lawyer present."

"This little problem is easy to solve," said Robbie. "You go on back to the office, Damon. Ruby Nell can call Fletcher." She turned to Ruby Nell. "Fletcher is your lawyer, isn't he?"

"Fletcher, Junior—Fletch," said Ruby Nell and sipped some more brandy.

"After Fletch gets here, the two of them can come to your office so you can ask your questions."

Damon raised his voice slightly. "We're talking a murder investigation here, Robbie, and I'm not sure how it will look."

"How what will look?"

"A request for a lawyer coming from the sheriff's house."

"Oh, for heaven sake's, Damon. That doesn't make

sense. People request lawyers from your office. What difference does it make?" Robbie took his arm, silently urging him to leave the room. "Besides, I don't care how it looks."

They walked out into the hallway.

"I meant how it might look legally," he said in a low tone.

"I know what you meant. I'm telling you it won't matter in the long run. Ruby Nell didn't kill her mother."

"And I suppose you're going to tell me how you know that."

"Not exactly. Damon, I've known Ruby Nell since I was six years old. She sacrificed her own happiness to take—"

"Maybe she finally got a bellyful. Maybe Mrs. Poteet wasn't the easiest person to get along with . . ."

"Damon," Robbie said. "You'll just have to take my word for it. I have no doubts about my friend." Damon followed as she pulled him further down the hallway.

"You're taking a strong stand here. I knew you and Ruby Nell were friends, but I didn't know you were close enough for you to go out on a limb for her."

"We don't pal around together, if that's what you mean. We were very close when we were younger. In recent years, I've been taking care of you and the kids, and she's been taking care of her mother, but that doesn't change the—"

"Honey, people do change. That's a fact of life."

"Yes, but there are things that happened a long time ago. Things I'm not at liberty to tell you, Damon. And because of what happened back then, I know she hasn't changed. And she would *not* kill her mother."

Damon started to speak, but Robbie put her hand over his lips. "You probably have evidence to the contrary, but there are some missing pieces that will tell you the truth. Go

184

back to the office," Robbie said. "Do what you have to do."

"What about lunch?"

"Stop at Jack-in-the-Box and get a salad. Just go on—get out of here."

Damon smiled in defeat, walked to the kitchen and out the back door.

Robbie listened until his Ford Bronco pulled out of their driveway and went down the street. Only then did she go back to the study.

Ruby Nell was on the telephone to Fletcher Frankowski, Jr. "Okay, Fletch, I'll meet you at the sheriff's office in thirty minutes. Bye."

"You get things worked out, Ruby Nell?"

"I think so. Robbie, I'm sorry I got hysterical. That's not like me."

"Don't think a thing about it. You've just lost your mother and—"

"I still don't understand any of this. I mean last night the nursing home called and said Mother had died. I've been expecting it. With the pneumonia and her other health problems. Naturally I assumed she'd died from natural causes. But this morning at the funeral home . . ." She wiped her eyes again with a Kleenex.

"It's going to be okay, Ruby Nell. But maybe you shouldn't go into any more details. What I don't know can't cause you any problems."

The women walked to the front of the house. "Are you going to be able to drive yourself?" Robbie asked.

"Oh, yes. I'm fine now. Thanks, Robbie. Goodness, I must look a fright. I'd better run on over to the house and freshen up before I meet the sheriff and Fletch Frankowski."

Robbie gave Ruby Nell a quick hug. "I know you didn't

have anything to do with your mother's death. I'm sure everything will work out."

"I hope so. And thanks again, Robbie." Ruby Nell Poteet got into her car and left.

Robbie returned to her computer and her almost completed manuscript, but she couldn't keep her mind on her story. The real-life drama of her childhood friend was all she could think about.

She and Ruby Nell Poteet had grown up four houses from each other in a neighborhood filled with boys. Ruby Nell was older, but the two girls became close, almost as close as sisters. They told each other secrets, things they could never tell anyone else.

Robbie was a mature girl probably because she was around adults most of her childhood and because her one close friend was older.

When Ruby Nell was thirteen and Robbie was nine, Ruby Nell had confided her most horrible secret. Robbie remembered that day in nineteen forty-seven as clearly as if it had happened last week.

Robbie Jo Jamison was sitting on a low branch of the chinaberry tree in her own back yard waiting for Ruby Nell. Ever since Mrs. Poteet got sick, Ruby Nell didn't get to come outside often.

Robbie didn't really mind waiting, but she was anxious to tell her friend a secret. "My mother's giving me a Toni on Saturday," Robbie would say, "and I'm scared it's gonna frizz up like last time." Ruby Nell had naturally curly red-gold hair that never needed a permanent like Robbie's straight brown hair did.

Ruby Nell wasn't yet too old for telling secrets to, although she was beginning to look like a lady, and she was getting those big-lady things on her chest.

186

"I'm getting a bustline," Ruby Nell had said.

Robbie knew they were called breasts, but nice young ladies didn't say those vulgar words.

Robbie heard someone running, and the sound grew louder as Ruby Nell burst around the corner of the Jamison's house and climbed up on a tree branch next to Robbie.

Robbie hadn't known, at first, that Ruby Nell was crying.

"I hate him. I hate him," sobbed Ruby Nell.

"Who?"

"My, uh, my father."

"Oh, Ruby Nell, you don't really mean it; you're not supposed hate your father. You love your father because—"

"I can't love him."

"Why?"

"I try and try, but I'm not Mamma."

"I know that, silly," said Robbie.

"But he comes and gets in my bed with me and kisses me and stuff."

"What's stuff?" Robbie wanted to know.

"Just stuff." Ruby Nell was still crying big drops and getting her blouse damp. "Oh, Robbie. He wants me to do nasty stuff, and I don't want to do it. He say he loves me and that if I love him, I'll let him kiss me and stuff."

Robbie didn't know what Ruby Nell was talking about. Fathers always love you, and her daddy gave her a good night kiss every night before she went to sleep. "I like for my daddy to give me a good night kiss."

"This is different. I can't explain it too good, you're just a little—"

"Don't you say I'm just a little girl. I hear that all the time, and I'm not. I'm almost as tall as you are."

"I don't mean . . . oh, never mind."

The girls sat silently for a little while, and suddenly Ruby

Nell started talking. "Robbie, if I tell you a big secret, do you promise not to tell?"

Robbie nodded.

"You've got to cross your heart and hope to die, stick a needle in your eye—if you ever tell."

"Okay," said Robbie, making a big X sign on her chest. "I cross my heart."

"You can't tell anyone."

"Not even my mother?"

"No one." Ruby Nell's voice got quiet. "Robbie? Have you ever seen your Daddy in the bathtub?"

Robbie nodded.

"Well, boys and men have a thing . . ."

"A penis. Mother told me it was a penis."

"Yes. And when grownups get married and they sleep together, sometimes the man puts it inside his wife."

"I know, mother told me. To make babies, but how can he put it there?"

"It's kinda hard to do until you're a grownup lady." Ruby Nell's voice lowered to a whisper. "My daddy puts his thing inside me at night and he kisses me."

"Every night?"

"Just about."

"He's not supposed to do that; he's your father."

"I know, but he says it's because he loves me. And he says if I tell Mama it will kill her. I don't want my mama to die. I hate him, and I don't want to love him anymore."

"Me either. I mean, I don't like him anymore."

Nineteen forty-six was the year Ruby Nell's mother gave birth to a stillborn baby boy. Mrs. Poteet went into a deep depression afterwards because she blamed herself for the loss of the baby. She became incapable of doing much more than getting out of bed once or twice a day to eat.

For the next year and a half, Ruby Nell took care of her mother, the meals, the laundry, the house and her father. Mr. Poteet expected Ruby Nell to perform all the wifely duties his wife was incapable of doing, including meeting his sexual needs.

It had all happened years before anyone talked about sexual abuse. The girls had not known that what Mr. Poteet was doing was sexual abuse, but they did know it was wrong. Unfortunately, they didn't know how to stop it or what to do about it.

Eventually, Mrs. Poteet came out of her depression and slowly regained an interest in what was going on in her home. With her improvement, it didn't take long for her to discover what had occurred between her husband and her daughter. Mr. Poteet adamantly refused to stop having sex with Ruby Nell. He said his daughter was his property to do with as he pleased. He planned to divorce his wife and run away with his daughter. Mrs. Poteet took matters into her own hands and Mr. Poteet died mysteriously.

The authorities were never able to prove anything, and no one ever knew the truth except Ruby Nell, her mother and Robbie.

Mrs. Poteet had killed her husband to save her daughter. Ruby Nell knew that her mother's love for her was powerful. For the rest of her life no matter what her mother asked of her or expected her to do, the daughter did, and did gladly.

Ruby Nell could never harm her mother because of the extraordinary bond between them. And because of the secret sworn between two little girls years ago, Robbie wouldn't tell Damon about it unless Ruby Nell gave her permission.

III

The late autumn sun was sinking behind a scrub cedar ridge as Sheriff Dunlap parked his Bronco in the parking lot at Adobe Creek Nursing Center and got out. He pulled his denim jacket tighter. They'd been having nice sunny days, but when evening came, things cooled off quickly.

He'd already questioned the late night crew who had been on duty when Mrs. Poteet died. It hadn't been easy and took most of the day, since many of them slept during daytime and those who weren't asleep held other jobs.

Damon took the elevator to the second floor nursing station and introduced himself to Sonja Walker, R.N. Mrs. Walker was the nurse who'd given the report at shift change, and Damon wanted to know if she had seen Ruby Nell Poteet come by to see her mother. During his questioning of the graveyard crew certain angles came up that he wanted to clarify.

One angle concerned Vanita Gomez, a nurse's aide who'd been on duty. Damon was determined to shed some light on what had really happened here last night.

Sonja Walker was about four feet ten and wouldn't weigh much over ninety pounds even when she was sopping wet, Damon thought. At his height he felt like a giant towering over her. He asked if they could talk in the employee lounge; that way he'd be able to sit down, and she wouldn't get a neck strain trying to look up at him.

Sonja, as she told him to call her, led the way. Her long brown hair was done up into a braid that his wife would know the name of, but he could only describe as an Indian girl braid. The braid swinging back and forth ahead of him came within his reach several times. He suppressed an urge

190

to pull it and felt as foolish as a ten-year-old.

By the time they were seated and the nurse had poured coffee for them, Damon had put thoughts of childish pranks aside and was back into his sheriff role. "Sonja, I've questioned everyone on duty last night, and only one employee, Vanita Gomez, admits seeing Ruby Nell Poteet come in to visit her mother."

"So I've heard."

"Did you see Ruby Nell?"

"No, I was giving my report and all I was concerned with was finishing that and getting the hell outta here." Her face turned a light shade of pink with the frank admission. "I do have another life besides Adobe Creek Nursing."

"I would imagine so."

"But I don't doubt what Vanita said about seeing Ruby Nell here last night. Ruby Nell often came by around dinner time in case we needed help in feeding Mrs. Poteet, and, after her mother turned critical, she usually came back later in the evening, too."

"Then it wasn't unusual for her to come after nine or ten o'clock?"

"Not at all."

"But isn't it odd that no one saw her except Vanita?"

"Not with shift change. When you've added extra people for thirty to forty-five minutes and everyone is trying to get patients settled down for the night, it can be chaotic." Sonja suddenly looked at him wide-eyed. "Are you accusing Vanita of something?"

In an investigation a sheriff has to keep a poker face occasionally. He'd heard things about Vanita while questioning the others. The woman herself admitted how she liked to be around when a patient died. She was somehow pleased about it. "I just have to tie up some of the loose ends," he said.

"And Vanita is one of your loose ends?"

"More or less," he said.

"In a way I'm not surprised. I hate to say it, but Vanita is a bit of an odd ball."

"Oh. How so?"

"Her attitude about death. Sometimes I honestly think that if she could do it legally, she'd personally send them on their way to glory."

All right, Damon thought. He'd been hoping someone would come out and say it. "I understand. I got that same idea when I talked to her."

Sonja said, "Don't get me wrong. She cares for the patients. Actually, she probably cares too much. And she does have a valid point when she says we put our animals to sleep to put them out of their misery, and why don't we do the same for old people? I agree with her for the most part."

"Could she decide to help someone along in the death struggle? Or would she?"

"If you're asking hypothetically, sure. Nurses working with terminal patients do have opportunities, but we don't take advantage. Or most of us don't. There have been cases right here in Texas where . . . but, you know all that. If you're asking if Vanita ever assisted a death, I couldn't swear one way or the other. I may have given a fleeting thought about her a time or two, but there was never anything I could prove. Never even anything I could report to a supervisor. It was just a gut instinct. Nothing more."

"How about the medical charts? Could someone look at those and discover a pattern or arrive at a conclusion?"

"I suppose, but I haven't done that." She got up and poured the last swallow of her coffee into the sink and rinsed out her mug. "I'm like most people who work here. I try to do the best job I can when I'm on duty, but when I leave, I leave. I don't want to think about this place or talk about it or anything else. It's the only way I can keep my sanity."

"Sounds like a healthy attitude."

"Well, I need my job, and I don't rock the boat even if I have a question in my mind sometime that Vanita is strange. I've never seen her harm anyone."

Damon knew he might be on shaky ground to get a court order to inspect the medical charts, but if he could come up with a reasonable way to get Sonja Walker to look, he might find enough for him to take to a judge.

"Sonja. I'm going to level with you. It will take a court order to go through those medical records. It's possible there is a pattern of actions about the woman. First thing Monday morning, I plan to ask Judge Smith to give me that court order."

He paused to see how she was taking it, and was mildly surprised to see the eagerness in Sonja's face. Somewhere down the line she's wondered about Vanita, he thought, but she's probably never expressed it out loud before. She wants to look at the records, too.

"Judge Smith has been known to delay a decision for two or three weeks on some whim or the other. In the meantime if Vanita Gomez becomes suspicious about me checking her out, she might decide to leave town. I can't legally look at them, but you can. And maybe while you're there I can look over your—"

"Let's go look then," Sonja said, interrupting him. "If Vanita is guilty of anything, I want to know about it. I want her stopped. The sooner, the better, before she gets us all into trouble."

Damon followed Sonja to the elevator. On the way she was interrupted by a commotion in a patient's room.

"Could you wait a moment?" Sonja asked.

Damon was prepared to cool his heels indefinitely, but the nurse didn't take more than two minutes.

"Mr. Jenkins," she said. "Keeps calling for his dead wife. He even tries to get up to go find her."

"He doesn't know?"

"Yes, but he doesn't remember."

Damon shuddered as they took the elevator downstairs to the basement. He hoped he'd never forget if something happened to Robbie.

Sonja guided him to row upon row of file cabinets. "This is going to take some time."

Damon thought that was an understatement.

IV

It was 9:00 p.m. when Sheriff Dunlap returned home. As soon as Damon walked in, Robbie could tell he had good news. If it hadn't been written all over his jubilant face, she could have told by his jaunty step and attitude. "You've found evidence to clear Ruby Nell?" she asked.

He grabbed Robbie into his arms and swung her off her feet. "Better than that. I've got another suspect. A strong suspect." Damon set her back on her feet and kissed her.

"Great. I guess can take your sleeping bag out of the doghouse now." She smiled up at him.

"Oh, ho. Is that where you were going to put me?"

"I was, unless you listened to the voice of reason." Robbie had worried all afternoon. Fletch Frankowski had called and admitted that after the talk at Damon's office, things looked bad for Ruby Nell. "I don't suppose you can discuss . . ."

"Not yet."

Damon looked in the oven to see what she had cooked for dinner. "Meat loaf. My favorite. Doesn't seem like you were too angry if you went to all that trouble."

"Even a condemned man deserves a favorite meal."

"You mean I was condemned already?"

"Being late almost ruined your dinner."

"Didn't Dispatch call? I asked them to call."

"They called, just in the nick of time, too. I was ready to put the meat loaf in the oven."

"So is all forgiven?"

"Don't push your luck." Robbie took a huge salad out of the icebox and mashed some potatoes. "Damon, there are things about Ruby Nell and her mother that I wasn't at liberty to tell you earlier today. I've since talked to Ruby Nell, and she says it's okay." The women had agreed that with Mrs. Poteet dead, it wouldn't hurt if Robbie told Damon.

"Robbie, I was only doing my job." Damon helped by setting the table. When the table was ready, he poured two glasses of iced tea and sat down.

"I know. That's why I wasn't really mad. I just got upset over Ruby Nell getting hysterical."

"So," he said. "Are you going to tell me what you couldn't tell me earlier?"

She put everything on the table and sat down, too. "Not right now. It's not very pleasant dinnertime conversation."

After dinner she told him.

Later, when they were in bed, Robbie said, "Damon? Will you hold me?"

He pulled her close. "What's wrong, Babe?"

"I think I'm a little down in the dumps. Thinking about Ruby Nell and the past. What she went through messed up her whole life, didn't it? She has never been able to relate to men. She's never known the wonder and joy of loving someone. And she'll never have children. It's all so sad."

"I keep thinking about you. You were so young to learn about Ruby Nell's abuse. It's a wonder you weren't warped emotionally."

"I probably would have been, but my mother was always open with me and talked to me. When I was nine she told me the facts of life and where babies came from. When I was twelve she talked about married love, and when I was thirteen she talked about how some men mistreat women. Looking back, I'm sure she suspected about the Poteets. I have to give my mom credit. She kept my head on straight."

"I've always thought your mom was special," he said. "Remind me to call and tell her that soon."

"Maybe now Ruby Nell can actually have a life. Find someone."

"Don't you think she's too old?"

"Damon. She's only five years older than I am, and we're not too old, are we?"

He laughed and patted her backside. "Not yet."

"Maybe she can find someone understanding."

"She'll probably have to go through counseling first."

"Well," Robbie said, "she needs to do that anyway. I'll encourage her along those lines. The rest will be up to the fates."

"Tonight, I only want to hold you close and comfort you, but does my fate include a little old-age excitement in the future?"

"Ask me again tomorrow morning."

On Sunday morning, Damon had an appointment to talk to the Adobe County D.A. When he returned home, he and Robbie took a drive out to the lake. Central Texas weather in the fall can be a perfect time to be outdoors, and they decided on a picnic.

Adobe Creek wasn't really a creek at all, although the small portion which ran through town was what most people would call a creek. It actually was a fork of the Texas Colorado River. About two miles west of town a dam had been built and a small lake had formed. It was a huge part of the town's attraction.

Picnic tables, camping sites and a small boat dock had been built on the side of the lake nearest the town. Robbie packed a lunch, and they ate and relaxed in lawn chairs under a live oak tree watching the water and a sailboat nearby. They didn't often have a chance for good leisure time together.

Robbie knew something weighed heavily on Damon's mind, although he tried to hide it and not let it spoil their day. She wasn't too surprised when he finally spoke.

"I've got bad news and bad news. The D.A. says we don't have enough evidence against our suspect to make an arrest."

"Well, at least Ruby Nell is cleared."

"That's the rest of my bad news. We found out this morning by an overnight fax there was an insurance policy on Thelma Poteet, and her daughter is the beneficiary. Ruby Nell stands to inherit $500,000 dollars."

"But that . . ."

"The D.A. says the odds of making a case against her just went sky high. Of course, he doesn't know what you and I know. Even if he did, an eye witness puts her in her mother's room, less than an hour before Mrs. Poteet was found dead. And if getting out from under her mother's tyranny wasn't enough, the money gives her a strong motive. He's in favor of us making an arrest. I've managed to stall him for another twenty-four hours."

"What are you going to do?"

197

"I'm not sure. Try to come up with stronger evidence against my other suspect, but I don't know if there's anything else to find."

They got up and walked down to the shoreline. Usually Robbie enjoyed the lake and the huge limestone boulders that hugged the edge in places. If the sunlight hit the rocks just right, it was possible to see minute particles of calcite glinting. Damon's news about the possible arrest of Ruby Nell put a damper on everything.

When Damon was in the mood to explore more thoroughly, he would look for fossils imbedded in the boulders. Today Robbie noticed he walked over the rocks without seeing them.

They walked arm in arm, except where the going was too rough, and then he would steady her. They reached the water's edge and stopped, standing on a flat limestone boulder.

"Damon, I've racked my brain trying to figure out who could have killed Thelma Poteet. Who even would want her dead." Robbie stepped down, almost slipped even with Damon supporting her, and was glad she'd worn her sneakers. "I know you don't like to say anything prematurely about your case, but even I can deduce a few things about the murderer."

"Let me hear your theory," he said. "It might help clarify my thinking."

"That insurance policy doesn't make any difference in my book. I still don't think Ruby Nell had enough motive to kill her mother. That means the only other people with access to Mrs. P. would be someone from the nursing home. But why would someone at Adobe Creek want to get rid of a sick old woman?"

"Good question. Do you have an answer?" He held out

his hand to help her and they sat down on the rock side by side.

"The only logical explanation is that Mrs. P. saw or heard something she wasn't supposed to."

"For instance?"

"How would I know?" She looked at him and saw his slight grin. "Oh, I see. You don't know either. What's wrong? Is it too difficult for you? You want me to try to solve your case?"

"I think I have it solved. I just want to hear your version."

"I don't have a version. I'm only thinking out loud," she said and punched him in the shoulder. "I've helped you solve cases before. I'm not a novice. Besides, I read and write mysteries and—"

"Fiction isn't real life."

"I know, and truth is stranger than fiction." She paused for a moment. "Look, did you see that fish jump over there?"

"Sure did. Wish I'd brought my fishing pole."

"Anyway, back to Mrs. P.'s death. Let's start with the premise that the old woman heard or saw something. Since I worked twenty years in X-ray, I know a little about what goes on in hospitals and nursing homes. I would make a guess that Mrs. P. saw someone stealing drugs or mistreating patients."

"You're getting warm there."

"The mistreatment part?"

"Along the right track, but a little different."

"Okay," Robbie said. "She saw someone doing something to a patient. That place is full of people who are terminal or will be before long. Did Mrs. P. see someone killing a patient to put them out of their misery?"

"Almost on the nose, Old Gal."

"Damon, if she saw a nurse or orderly kill a patient, she was in jeopardy. Maybe that explains why she got pneumonia in the first place."

Damon stood up and began pacing beside the boulder. "Whoa, I hadn't thought of that."

"What if a nurse or orderly injected her with a pneumococcal virus, and when that didn't work fast enough, she was smothered."

"This raises some possibilities I need to check out." He strode off, taking the shortest path, which happened to also be one of the roughest. "I've got to get back to town, Robbie."

"Wait a minute, you big lug. You better not go off and leave me." She stood and started after him.

"Okay," he said and went back to help her. "But we need to hurry. I've got to check something out."

Later that evening, a friend of Robbie's named Iona Winston called to say she had fallen while visiting in Austin and had broken her hip. The doctors had fixed her up, and Iona said she was doing fine, although she still needed nursing care and some physical therapy treatments. Her daughter lived in Oklahoma City, worked as a teacher and also had small children.

The only solution was for Iona to check into Adobe Creek Nursing until she was able to care for herself. She asked if Robbie would bring some fresh clothes and toilet items to her, and Robbie said she would.

Robbie was already asleep when Damon came in, well after midnight. She roused herself briefly when he got into bed.

"Tomorrow I'll grab breakfast out someplace and head back over to the nursing home," he said. "This case is driving me crazy. Everything I come up with falls apart. Nothing makes sense."

The next morning Robbie finished the final draft of her manuscript. At eleven, she went to visit Iona Winston at Adobe Creek Nursing Home, stopping by Iona's house first to pick up the necessary requested items.

Robbie parked in the visitors' lot at Adobe Creek and went inside. It had been a while since she'd been to the home, and she was pleased to see some of the redecorating changes that had taken place since her last trip. New paint, wallpaper, and furniture had brightened everything. A noticeable difference was the center didn't have that odor of old age and illness anymore. The new administrator had improved the place tremendously. Robbie couldn't help wondering what the adverse publicity might do if an employee was arrested for the murder of Thelma Poteet.

At the second floor nursing station, Robbie reported she was visiting Mrs. Winston, in Room 202. When she reached the room, she realized it was the same one Thelma Poteet had occupied.

When Robbie walked into the room Iona Winston had her eyes closed, but opened them at the sound of footsteps. Iona looked exhausted, and her eye were bloodshot.

"Robbie, I've got to get out of this place. You've got to help me."

"What's wrong, Iona?"

"There's a crazy man in here. He came in my room last night, yelling and calling me a whore. He tried to smother me."

"For heaven's sake, Iona! How did you stop him?"

"I fought him off and finally got hold of the call bell and rang for the nurse. One of the aides came in and said for me not to get upset. That it was all a mistake."

"Don't get upset?" I said. "That crazy man tried to kill me!"

"Who was it? And why did he come in here?"

"Johnson, Jenkins. Something like that. He kept calling for Maureen. Calling her a whore and said he was going to kill me. He must have thought I was Maureen. Whoever she was. He had his hands around my neck for a moment. I managed to shove him away. He yanked the pillow out from under my head and tried to put it over my face."

"How horrible."

"Yes, it was, and I shudder to think what might have happened if he had been able to mash just a little harder on that pillow. Or if I hadn't been able to reach that call bell. I would be lying here dead now instead of talking to you."

The implication of her words grabbed at Robbie. "So that's how Mrs. Poteet was killed," she said.

Her friend looked puzzled. "What did you say?"

"Iona, I need to use your telephone to call Damon. Then I'm going to call your daughter and tell her to come down here to get you. I'll stay here with you until she comes."

"Oh, thank you, Robbie. Now maybe I can get some sleep. I wasn't able to sleep a wink last night after all that." Iona closed her eyes.

"No, thank *you*, Iona." Robbie patted her friend's arm, picked up the telephone and dialed. When Damon answered she said, "I've just solved the case for you . . . What? . . . Oh, I'm at Adobe Creek Nursing Center. I'm going to hang up now and call Ruby Nell. I've got to let her know her ordeal is over."

A Front Row Seat

I awoke on that cold wet March morning with a fierce sinus headache over my right eye. Things went downhill from there. I broke a fingernail and tore a run in my pantyhose. I had to dress twice because I snagged my sweater and had to change. When I walked out the front door I banged my little toe against the potted plant I'd brought inside for protection from the cold. "Damn Sam." I limped out to my car and sank into the seat gratefully.

Some mornings should be outlawed, I thought, but I managed to get to the office which I own and operate with my partner, Cinnamon Jemima Gunn, at eight-thirty a.m. on the dot. C.J., as she's know to all except a few close friends, would have killed me if I'd opened up late. With the way things were going, death didn't sound half bad.

At nine a man pushed opened the door with its distinctive sign, G. & G. Investigations. He stopped cold in the middle of the reception area and looked around as if searching for someone.

He wasn't handsome. His nose was too long, and it hooked at the end, ruining his overall attractiveness. Dark, blue-black hair waved across his head and curled down over the tips of his ears. His eyes were blue-gray, and crinkle lines radiated outward from the corners. He was probably no taller than five feet ten with a rounded abdomen and torso, like he'd rather sit in front of the tube and vege out than work out. I'd guess his age around fifty.

"May I help you?" I asked.

His navy suit looked expensive, but off-the-rack, and

he'd added a floral print tie to spiff up his white shirt. He wore a black London Fog-style raincoat, open and unbelted, and a perplexed look.

"Do you need an investigator?" I asked when he didn't answer my first question.

"Is Mr. Gunn here?" His voice was husky, like he had a cold.

"There is no Mr. Gunn. Only C.J., but she's in court."

"She? I don't understand. I want to talk to Mr. C.J. Gunn." His annoyance was obvious in his derisive tone.

"C.J. isn't a Mister. C.J.'s a woman."

"I'll speak to your boss, then."

"I'm it." I smiled. "I mean, I own this agency. Well, C.J. and I are co-owners actually. I'm Jenny Gordon."

"You mean this detective agency is run by a bunch of damn women?"

"That's about it, sir."

"Well, shit." He turned, walked out and slammed the door.

"Up yours, fella," I said to his retreating footsteps.

I didn't waste time wondering about him. It happened occasionally—some macho pea-brain unable to hire a female private eye because of his own ego. I shrugged and turned back to the computer terminal.

Electronic technology baffles me. I think I'm a little intimidated to think a machine is smarter than I am. But C.J., who's a computer whiz, had set up a program for our business invoices, and all I had to do was fill in the blanks, save, and print. I could handle that much.

G. & G.'s bank account was dangerously low. Unless we collected on some delinquent accounts or came up with a rich client or two, we were in deep do-do.

We'd worked too hard for that, but it meant sending out timely statements and following up with telephone calls.

Our biggest headaches were large insurance companies who always seemed to run sixty to ninety days past due.

I got all the blank spaces filled on the next account and saved the file, but before I could push the button to print, the telephone rang.

"Ms. Gordon, this is Dr. Anthony Randazzo." The husky voice was familiar. "I want to apologize for the way I acted a few minutes ago."

So, the piggy chauvinist was a doctor. His name rang a bell in my head, but I couldn't connect it. My first impulse was to hang up in his ear, but he kept talking fast—as if he could read my mind.

"Ms. Gordon, I've been under a lot of stress . . ." He laughed, sounding nervous, not jovial. "Boy, does that sound trite or what?"

I waited, unsure if he expected an answer.

"I honestly am sorry for storming out of your office. I acted like some idiot with a caveman mentality. I need an investigator, and your firm was highly recommended."

I'm not a die-hard feminist, but the emotional side of my brain was yelling *hang up on this bastard* while the practical left brain was reminding me we needed a paying client and the doctor could be one. I wondered who was wicked enough to send this clown in our direction. "May I ask who recommended you?"

"My niece works as a receptionist for Will Martin's law firm."

Oh, hell. Will and Carolyn Martin were counted among my closest friends. Good friends aren't supposed to send the jerks of the world to you.

"I've never met Mr. Martin," he continued, "but my niece thinks highly of him."

Whew! That explained it. When asked, Will automatically would have said, "G & G." Knowing this guy wasn't a client of Will's made me feel better. "Dr. Randazzo, perhaps I should refer—"

"Please, Ms. Gordon, don't judge me too quickly. My wife and I desperately need help. It's a matter of life or death."

Now that he was contrite he was much easier to take, but I still wasn't sure I wanted to work with him. "I'm not—"

"Please don't say no yet. Let me explain briefly. Two months ago, I was involved in a malpractice suit. You probably heard about it."

The bell in the back of the old brain pinged. Anyone old enough to read or watch television had heard. Because of the high costs of health care nowadays which the medical profession tried to blame on things like malpractice suits, the media had talked of nothing else. Randazzo was a plastic surgeon. A woman had sued him for ruining her face. She hadn't looked too bad on TV, but the jury awarded her a huge amount. Mostly for pain and anguish, as I recalled. The doctor had lost and lost big.

"Yes, I recall," I said, wondering why he needed a P.I. now. "But the lawsuit's over, isn't it?"

"Yes. Except for working out the payment schedule." He cleared his throat. "But I think our problem has a definite connection. I'm really worried and will be happy to pay a consulting fee for your time."

"I, uhmmm . . ."

"Would five hundred be appropriate?"

He got my attention. Five big ones would certainly help our bank account. I could probably work for Attila the Hun for five hundred dollars. Okay, so I can be bought. "Would you like to make an appointment?"

"If you're free this evening, my wife and I are having a

few friends over for drinks and hors d'oeuvres. If you and Ms. Gunn could join us—whatever you decide to do afterwards is entirely up to you, but the five hundred is yours either way."

"What time?"

"Seven, and thanks for not hanging up on me."

Dr. Randazzo gave me directions to his house, and we hung up.

I had the invoices ready to mail by the time C.J. returned.

She remembered the Randazzo lawsuit. "Five hundred dollars just to talk?"

"That's what the man said."

"Are you sure he's not kinky?" A knowing look was on her cola nut-colored face, and her dark eyes gleamed wickedly.

"Maybe. But he said his wife and other people would be there. It didn't sound too kinky."

"Hummm. Guess the lawsuit didn't bankrupt him if he's got five C notes to throw around." C.J. worked her fingers across the computer keyboard.

"He probably has hefty malpractice insurance," I said.

I watched as she punched keys and letters appeared on the monitor in front of her eyes. C.J. can find out the most illuminating information about people in only a matter of minutes. With my technology phobia I don't understand modems, networks and E-mail and have no idea what it is that she does. I've also decided I really don't want to know any details.

"Let's just check on his finances. I'm sure he has investments, stocks and bonds, real estate and what have you. Never knew a doctor who didn't." A few minutes later she muttered an "Ah-ha. Looks like Randazzo was shrewd enough to put a nice nest egg into his wife's name, but his medical practice is close to bankruptcy." She printed up some figures, stuck the papers in a folder, and we closed the office and left.

Since my apartment is only a few blocks from our office and her place is halfway across town, C.J. keeps a few clothes and essentials there for convenience. We took turns showering and dressing.

C.J. wanted to drive. Since she liked to change cars about every six months, she'd recently leased a Dodge Dakota SE pickup truck, as roomy and as comfortable as a car. But what she was proudest of was a fancy sound system, tape deck and CD player. She popped a CD in and turned up the volume.

A woman sang, "I wanna be around to pick up the pieces, when somebody breaks your heart."

"All riiight." I laughed, and she raised an eyebrow. I picked up the box and read about the songs and the artists. These were golden oldies by: Peggy Lee, Nancy Wilson, Sarah Vaughn, Judy Garland and others. It wasn't her usual type of music.

"That's Dinah Washington," she said. "I knew you were gonna get a kick out of this one."

I'd been hooked on country music forever, but a couple years ago I discovered Linda Ronstadt singing ballads from the 30s and 40s. And the funny thing is, I remember my parents playing records and dancing to music like this. It's an early memory and a rare one with my parents having fun. Somehow my mother's long unsuccessful battle with cancer had wiped out too many good memories.

I listened to Dinah singing about her old love getting his comeuppance, and how sweet revenge can be while she's sitting and applauding from a front row seat.

"Cripes," I said. "That really knocks me out. I've gotta have a copy."

"I'll give you this one, Girl, after I've listened to it."

The Randazzos' house was located in the hills above Lake Travis, west of Austin. After a couple of wrong turns we found the brick pillars which flanked the entrance of the long drive. The blacktop curved to the front of the house and ended in a concrete parking area. C.J. pulled up between a dark green Jaguar and a tan Volvo.

The Spanish-modern house was large and rambling, made of tan brick with a burnt sienna tile roof and built onto the side of a hill. The arched windows were outlined in the same color tile as the roof, and black wrought-iron bars covered the bottom halves. The Saint Augustine grass was a dun-muckle brown with little shoots of green poking out—normal for this time of year.

We got out and walked up to the ornately carved double doors. I pushed the oval lighted button beside the facing.

"Some joint," C.J. said as we waited.

A young man dressed in a cable-knit sweater with a Nordic design and charcoal gray slacks opened the door. Late twenties, blond and blue eyed with a Kevin Costner smile, he was so handsome my breath caught in my throat.

When I said Dr. Randazzo expected us, he frowned but stepped back and said, "Come in."

We were in an entry hall which ran across most of the width of the front and was open ended on both sides. I couldn't recall ever seeing a house where you entered into a width-wise hallway.

We were directly in front of and looking into a large square atrium. Behind the glass wall was a jungle of green plants, shrubs and trees, with a spray of water misting one side. The darkening sky was visible through the roof, and I saw a couple of small green birds flitting back and forth between some trees.

The scene was exquisite. Several moments passed before I could find my voice. "I-I'm Jenny Gordon, and this is C.J. Gunn. We were to see Dr. Randazzo at seven."

"I'm Christopher Lansen, and I work with Tony Randazzo." His voice was nasal and high-pitched; it sure didn't go with his looks. "And I'm sorry, Tony isn't here at the moment."

"Oh?" I asked. "A medical emergency?"

"I don't think so. I mean, I don't know exactly."

"I'm sure Tony will be back shortly. Please come in," said a woman coming into the hall from the right side. Her voice was soft, and there was no trace of a Texas accent. She sounded as if she'd had elocution lessons and had graduated at the top of the class.

She was dressed in a soft blue silk shirtwaist dress, belted with a gold chain, and wore gold hoop gypsy earrings. She was tall and willowy with dark hair pulled severely back into a bun. She would have looked elegant except she hunched her shoulders instead of standing straight.

She had high cheekbones and almond-shaped dark eyes. There was a hint of Spanish or American Indian in her tight, unlined and unblemished face. Her age could have been anywhere from thirty to sixty. Probably has had a facelift, I thought.

"I'm Marta Randazzo. Are you the investigators my husband hired?"

"Uh . . . yes," I said. "And please call me Jenny. My partner is C.J."

The young man put his hand on her arm. "Marta, why don't you go back inside and I'll talk—"

"No, Chris. I, I want to speak to them now." Her voice sounded tentative, as if she hated to contradict him. She turned abruptly and walked down the hallway towards the left, leaving us no choice except to follow.

"Mrs. Randazzo," said C.J., who was walking directly behind the woman. "I should clarify something. Your husband asked us over for a consultation only. He hasn't actually hired us."

Marta Randazzo entered a huge den/family room. At least half of my apartment could fit into this one room, but maybe it seemed bigger because of the glass wall of the atrium. Another wall was taken up by a fireplace large enough to roast a side of beef. The room's decor was in Southwestern Indian colors. Navajo rugs and wall hangings, Kachina dolls, framed arrowhead and spear points, Zuni pottery, turquoise and silver jewelry knickknacks were everywhere. In a small alcove to one side of the fireplace was a wet bar. A sofa, love seat and three chairs were covered in Indian-design fabrics.

It felt like deja vu until I remembered I'd once been in a living room decorated with Indian things. Inexplicably, I couldn't remember when or where. "It's a lovely room," I told her. "I like it."

"Thank you." She motioned for us to sit, indicating the sofa, and she sat on a chair to our right. Christopher Lansen took a spot standing near the fireplace.

"I believe Chris told you Tony isn't here at the moment," Marta said. "He should be back soon."

But she didn't sound too certain. "I'm sure . . . I, uh, know he didn't forget you were coming . . ."

Chris Lansen said, "Marta, I don't think—"

"Chris?" Marta Randazzo stiffened. "Let me finish, please."

Lansen turned away and walked to the window, staring out into the darkness. His body language indicated he didn't like something she'd said or was about to say.

"Tony mentioned you were coming." Marta got up, walked to the mantle, ignoring Lansen, and took a piece of paper out from under a Zuni bowl. "He had me write out a check for you." She walked over and held it out to me.

I automatically reached for the paper and looked at her. I glimpsed a flicker of something in her eyes just before she turned and sat down, but then it was gone. Fear maybe? Or despair. I couldn't be sure.

The check was made out to G. & G. Investigations for five hundred dollars and signed by Marta Randazzo.

"Mrs. Randazzo," said C.J. "Perhaps we should wait until your husband returns and we can talk to him."

"I agree," said Chris. He looked at Marta with a stern expression. Some battle of wills was going on between the two of them. "He'll be back soon." Lansen's tone was emphatic. "He and I planned to talk about the surgery I'm doing on Mrs. Franklin tomorrow. He wouldn't forget about that."

"Oh, you're a doctor, too?" I asked, hoping to ease the tension. He and Marta were definitely uptight.

"Yes. I'm an associate of Tony's. A junior partner."

"We could wait a little while for him if it won't inconvenience you, Mrs. Randazzo." I tried to hand the check back to her. She ignored it, so I placed it on the end table next to me.

"Please, call me Marta," she said. She jutted her chin slightly. "That check means you are working for me, doesn't it?"

"We're here on consult. That was my agreement with Dr. Randazzo."

"Then, in that case, I'm consulting you. It must be obvious to you both . . . I should explain."

Chris Lansen cleared his throat and Marta Randazzo looked at him, her face creased with a frown. Her chin jutted out again briefly before she relaxed. "Jenny, C.J.? Would you like something to drink? Coffee or something stronger?"

"Coffee would be fine," said C.J., and I agreed.

"Chris? Would you go make coffee for my guests?" Her tone sounded like an order, but she didn't raise her voice.

He gave her a look as if she'd just asked him to wash the windows or something equally distasteful, but he left the room without speaking.

"Jenny, my husband has disappeared," she said when Lansen was gone. "I was taking a shower. After I dressed and came out here, Tony was gone. I assumed he'd gone for a walk, but that was at five o'clock, and he still isn't back yet."

"Have you looked for him?" I asked. She reminded me of someone, but I didn't know who.

"Yes. Chris came over about six and when I mentioned I was getting worried about Tony, Chris got into his car and drove around looking. He didn't find Tony."

"Your husband walks regularly?" C.J. asked.

"Yes, if something is bothering him. It's his way of relieving stress. But he's usually back after about twenty to thirty minutes."

"Could his disappearance have something to do with why he wanted to hire us?" I noticed out of the corner of my eye that C.J. was poised on the edge of her seat.

C.J. got up, muttering something about going to help with the coffee and went in the same direction Chris had gone. I knew she was using the old divide-and-question-separately technique.

"Maybe," said Marta.

"Do you know why he—"

"Yes," said Marta. "Someone's trying to kill me."

"What makes you think someone is trying to kill you?"

"Someone followed me all last week. The same man I think, I'm sure it was the same car." She began twisting the hem of her skirt as she talked, and I noticed bruises on her inner thigh near her left knee.

"After I became aware of this man," she continued, "I realized he'd probably followed me even before that. Then night before last that same car tried to run me car off the road. You drove up here and saw those treacherous curves. And the cliffs are pretty steep. I almost went over the edge. It scared me silly."

"Why would anyone want you dead?"

"I don't know, uh . . . maybe it's someone from the Davis family—wanting to get back at Tony."

"The Davis family?"

"The people who sued my husband."

"But why? They won their case."

C.J. and Chris came back into the room. He was carrying a silver serving tray with four china cups sitting in saucers.

Chris said, "My thoughts exactly. Why would anyone from the Davis family—"

"Money might not be enough," said C.J.

"What?" asked Marta.

"Revenge can be sweeter than money." C.J. sat on the sofa where she'd been before while Chris placed the tray on the coffee table. "Mrs. Davis feels she has suffered," she said. "And now it's Mrs. Randazzo who must suffer."

Chris carefully handed a saucered cup of coffee to each of us and then took his and returned to the fireplace. "That's what Tony thought," he said placing his coffee on the mantle. "But I think it's all hogwash."

"I know what you think, Chris. You've been vocal enough about it." Marta's voice got lower, and that made her words sound more ominous. "You think I'm imagining all this, but you don't know. You just don't know." Marta began stirring her coffee, banging the spoon against the cup. "Tony believed me. And now something has happened to him."

"Oh, Marta," said Chris with a *there, there, little lady* tone. "Tony's only been gone a couple of hours. He's gotten sidetracked, that's all."

"Maybe he twisted his ankle and fell into one of the canyons," I said. "He could even be unconscious."

"I looked in all the likely places," said Chris.

"Maybe you should call the search and rescue squad," I said.

"Law enforcement won't be inclined to do anything until he's been missing for twenty-four hours or so," said C.J.

"I want to hire you to find my husband and find out who . . ."

The doorbell rang and Chris, without asking Marta, left to answer it. He acted as if this were his house, not hers.

"Will you try to find Tony?" Marta asked, ignoring the interruption.

C.J. and I glanced at each other, and I saw her imperceptible nod of agreement.

"Okay, Mrs. Randazzo," I said. "You've just hired us." I picked up the check. "Consider this a retainer for two days."

My partner, who believes in being prepared, said, "I

have a contract with me." She pulled papers out of her shoulder bag, handed a page to Marta Randazzo who scanned it quickly, took the pen C.J. offered, and signed it.

"Marta?" I asked. "Does one of the cars out front belong to your husband?"

"The Jag is his. My Caddy is in the garage."

"And the Volvo belongs to Chris?"

Marta nodded.

Chris walked in with a man and woman trailing behind. The man was stocky, about fifty with heavy dark eyebrows and a hairline that receded back past his ears. The strands left on top were plastered to his reddish scalp. He was dressed in a three-piece suit and looked as if he'd rather be anyplace else except here. He walked straight to the bar without speaking and poured a drink.

The woman came over to where Marta now stood. "Chris told us Tony is missing." She was short with a voluptuous figure and blonde Farrah Fawcett hair. "Oh, Marta, you poor dear." The woman put her arms around Marta and kissed the air near Marta's cheek.

"I'm fine, Sonja." Marta recoiled from the woman's touch, but forced a smile. "I'm sorry, the party is canceled. Chris was supposed to call you."

"Oh, he came by about six-thirty. Said he was looking for Tony," said the woman. "He called back later and left a cancellation message on the infernal machine. I just thought we'd drop by on our way out to eat."

The woman noticed C.J. and me for the first time. She looked at Marta and said in a stage whisper as if we weren't there, "Are they from the police?"

"No, uh, Sonja Bernard." She nodded, and we stood. "This is Jenny Gordon and C.J. Gunn. They're private investigators."

The man who'd come in swayed over, a double shot of amber liquid in a glass. I assumed he was Sonja Bernard's husband.

"Private dicks, huh?" he said and laughed uproariously at his unfunny joke. From his slurred words it was obvious this drink was not his first. "Don't think I've ever met a female dick before, black or white. How do?" He took a big swallow and said, "Tough gals, huh? Do you carry guns? Which one is the dyke? I'll bet it's the black one."

"Bernie, don't be crude," said Sonja. "Their sexual preference is none of your damn business."

Marta's face turned red. "I apologize . . ."

I hated it too, because I knew C.J.'s sharp tongue would slash and trash Bernie before he could stagger another step. And that was if she decided to only chew him up instead of knocking him on his can. My partner's an ex-police woman, six feet tall and trained in Tukong Martial Arts. She could put him down and out.

I felt her body tense and spoke quickly, "C.J.? We probably should go." But I wasn't quite fast enough.

"He doesn't bother me, Mrs. Randazzo," said C.J. She smiled sweetly at the man, and then back at Marta. "His whiskey-soaked minuscule brain is ruled by his own penile inadequacy." Her next words were directed to me and spoken through clenched teeth. "You're right, Jenny. We must be on our way, but perhaps Marta will show us out. I have a couple more questions."

"What did she say?" asked Bernie. "Did she just insult me?"

"Of course, Bernie," said Chris, who walked over and took the man's arm. "But turnabout's fair play, wouldn't you say? Let's refresh your drink." Chris took the man's arm and turned him towards the bar.

The man needed another drink like a cowboy needed a burr under his saddle, but the maneuver had moved him out of C.J.'s reach.

The man followed, muttering something about how he'd bet a hundred dollars Tony was shacked up with a blonde someplace.

"I'm terribly embarrassed," said Sonja.

"And I'm terribly sorry for you," I said to her.

Marta Randazzo looked as if she'd like to climb into a hole someplace, but she walked out of the room instead.

C.J. and I followed. Marta veered off into a small sitting room where we stood and asked our questions.

C.J. made notes as Marta gave us descriptions of the car and the man who had followed her. She hadn't seen the license number. She said the people who sued her husband were Ellen and Herbert Davis.

"First," said C.J., "we'll check the local hospitals and emergency clinics, in case Dr. Randazzo has been brought in unconscious. And we'll try to check up on who's been following you. It won't be easy without that plate number."

"Will you call? No matter how late?" Marta asked. "I mean even if the news is . . ."

"Yes," I said. "We'll call if we hear anything." She gave us a recent photo of her husband.

"This could turn into an all night job," I said as we got into the truck and headed to town.

"Did you catch that last remark from old Bernie?" I asked.

"No, I was having too much trouble trying to keep from decking the guy."

"I figured. Bernie mumbled something about Tony being shacked up someplace."

"Which is why the police are reluctant to get involved in

domestic squabbles," said C.J. "The missing usually turn up the next day looking sheepish."

"Did you learn anything from Chris?"

"Only that he knew his way around the kitchen."

"You think the Randazzos quarreled?"

"Didn't you see the bruises on Marta's neck?"

"No, I missed those, but I saw bruises on her leg. That muddies up the waters a bit, doesn't it?"

The next morning we drove to work separately in our respective vehicles. My partner is a morning person and her energy and excitement greeting a new day bugs the hell out of me. I needed time for my body to wake up slowly, and the short drive without her helped.

Last night we'd checked all the emergency rooms without turning up the doctor. I'd called a friend, Jana Hefflin, who worked in Austin Police Department communications to see if her department had taken a call regarding a John Doe of anyone fitting Dr. Randazzo's description. She checked with the 911 operators, the EMS operators and police dispatch, all at APD headquarters. It was a negative on our man.

Finally, I called Marta Randazzo to report that there was nothing to report. It was almost two a.m. when we made up the bed in the guest room for C.J. and called it a night.

The new day was filled with sunshine and blue skies—reminding me of why I love central Texas.

Austin's built over the Balcones Fault, an ancient geological plate that eons ago rumbled and formed the hills, canyons and steep cliffs around west Austin. The land west of Austin is known as the Texas Hill Country. The city's east side slopes into gentle rolling hills and fertile farm land. Our office is in the LaGrange building which sits on a small knoll in far west Austin near the Mo-Pac Freeway. From our fourth floor office there's a fantastic view of limestone cliffs and small canyons to the west.

At the office, C.J. ran computer checks on the Davises. Ellen Davis had never sued anyone before, and neither she nor her husband had a police record. She also ran three other names: Sonja and Hirum "Bernie" Bernard and Christopher Lansen.

Mr. Bernard had a DUI and a resisting arrest charge pending. He also had a couple of business lawsuits resulting in settlements. Sonja Bernard had called the police recently in regard to a domestic dispute. Dr. Lansen had one bad debt on his credit record and a couple of unpaid parking tickets. A bunch of ordinary people, nothing to set off any alarm bells.

C.J. learned from a friend on the computer network that Ellen and Herbert Davis had left three weeks ago on an extended vacation to Hawaii. "That lets them out as revenge seekers," she said.

"You got that right," I said, using one of her favorite sayings. I called Mrs. Randazzo to see if she'd heard anything. She hadn't, and afterwards I made follow-up calls to the hospitals.

I told C.J. a trip to Dr. Randazzo's office might be helpful. "Maybe the doctor has a girlfriend, and someone from his office knows about it."

"Maybe he even plays with someone from work."

Having spent a few years around doctors myself, I knew the long hours of togetherness sometimes bred familiarity. "This whole thing just doesn't make good sense to me. If Randazzo and his wife had an argument and he stormed out, why didn't he go off in his Jag, not just head out on foot someplace?"

"Unless," said C.J., "he wanted to stage a disappearance. That malpractice suit left him in bad shape financially except for those assets in his wife's name."

I liked it. "What if he has other assets, hidden ones, and worked out a scheme? What better way than just walk off? Leave everything. And if another woman is involved she could meet up with him later. Intriguing, huh?"

"Yeah, but what about someone trying to kill Marta? If the Davises are out spending their newfound money, then who?"

"So," I said, "Randazzo hired someone to scare Marta in order to throw suspicion off of his own plans."

We couldn't come up with any more ideas, so I left to talk to the doctor's employees.

Randazzo's office was in the Medical/Professional high-rise building next door to Seton Hospital on Thirty-eighth Street, a few miles north of downtown and only a fifteen-minute drive from my office.

Years ago, I had worked at an X-ray clinic in this building. My husband, Tommy, used to pick me up for lunch, and we'd go around the corner to eat chicken-fried steak. The restaurant went bust a while back, and of course, Tommy was killed a couple of years ago. Nothing stays the same, I thought, as I pulled into an empty parking spot and got out.

Randazzo's suite of offices were on the second floor. A typical doctor's suite. Comfortable chairs in the waiting room, popular magazines scattered on tables and modernistic art prints hanging on the wall. A curly-top redheaded young woman, about eighteen, sat in the glassed-in cubicle.

Were receptionists getting younger or was I only getting older? After I explained who I was and what I wanted, I was asked to wait. Ms. Williams, the head nurse, would be with me in just a few minutes, I was told.

It was a good half hour before Ms. Williams called me. Her office was small, more like a closet under the stairs, but there was a desk and secretary-type chair. A telephone and a computer sat on the desk, and file folders covered all the remaining space. She was about my age of thirty-five, and every year showed on her face today. I'd guess a missing boss could upset routines.

"Ms. Williams, I'm sorry to bother you, but if you'll answer a few questions, I'll get out of your way."

"Please call me Tiffany. Ms. Williams reminds me of my mother, and I'd just as soon not think of her."

"I hear that," I said. "And I'm Jenny." Even though she didn't ask me to, I sat down. "I don't know if you've talked to Mrs. Randazzo today, but she's hired my partner and me to try to find her husband."

"Wow, I've never talked to a private detective before. It must be exciting." Tiffany Williams ran her hand through her brown hair which was cut extremely short and was two shades lighter than my own chestnut color.

"It's not exactly like it is on TV. Most of my work involves checking backgrounds on people. Nothing too exciting there."

She looked disappointed. "Dr. Lansen told us Mrs. Randazzo had hired someone to try to locate Dr. Tony. How do you go about finding a missing person?"

"Pretty much like I'm doing now with you. You talk to friends, family and co-workers. See if they have any knowledge or ideas."

"I don't know where he's gone. I just work here."

"I understand. But sometimes co-workers overhear things, and that chance remark might give a clue." She nodded and I continued, "Tell me about Dr. Randazzo."

"Tell you what?"

"What kind of boss is he? It helps if I can get some feel for the person. Did he seem unusually upset or worried about anything lately?"

"He's always upset about something. He's a very intense person. A control freak. He got upset whenever people wouldn't do as he said."

"You mean his patients?"

"Everyone. His wife, his employees, the hospital staff." Tiffany Williams began chewing her fingernails. They looked red and ragged, as if she'd already spent a lot of time gnawing. "Everyone is afraid of him, and no one would knowingly cross him—about anything."

"When I worked in X-ray I ran across doctors like that, and I always called it the prima-donna syndrome. Some doctors let a little power go to their heads." Tiffany was nodding in agreement after her initial surprise that I'd once worked in medicine.

"Yes. And when a second doctor comes in and is so nice, you see how things could be."

"You mean Dr. Lansen?"

"Yeah, he's so easygoing, but a great doctor, too. The patients all love him and the employees, too." She thought a moment. "I think everyone responds to his kindness, but that didn't go over with Dr. Tony."

"I can imagine. Do you know how Marta Randazzo got along with Dr. Lansen?"

"I don't know if I should say. It's not professional."

"I understand, and I don't blame you. Let me tell you what I've observed and see if you agree." She nodded and I said, "There's an undercurrent of something between them. It goes deeper than an—"

"Very definitely," she interrupted. "I think Chris hopes

to get ahead by being attentive to Marta."

"That doesn't sound too smart or ethical."

"I never said Chris is an angel. He has his faults. He wants a partnership with Dr. Tony, and he wants to reach the top as quickly as possible."

Okay, I thought, the young Dr. Lansen is ambitious. But was that enough to have caused Randazzo's disappearance? "How did Tony feel about Chris's ambitions?"

"Pleased as long as Chris kept Marta occupied."

"Oh?"

"Our patients are mostly female, and women find Dr. Tony's bedside manner quite charming. If Marta's attention was elsewhere then . . ." Realizing she was saying too much, she stood. "I've got to get back to work. It's gonna be one of those days."

I stood also. "Okay, but one more question. Was there one lady Dr. Tony was especially close to lately?"

She walked to the door, looking as if she were a little girl who'd just tick-a-locked her mouth shut. She then sighed. "I probably shouldn't, but you'll find out anyway if you keep digging. Dr. Tony is having a relationship with a patient—or was. We all knew about it."

"Who?"

"Sonja Bernard, a neighbor of theirs. He did surgery on her, and they got involved a few months ago. They were going hot and heavy, and it was beginning to get sticky."

"Did Marta know?"

She nodded. "Chris let it slip, but I'm sure it wasn't by accident. Chris always does things for a reason." Tiffany went out into the hallway. "I really do have to get busy."

"Okay and thanks." I turned to leave, but remembered something she'd just said. "You said Dr. Tony and Sonja were going hot and heavy?"

224

"Yes, but they broke up last week. And remember you didn't hear any of this from me."

"My lips are sealed."

On my way back to the office I wondered why Lansen had wanted Marta to know about Tony and Sonja. Somehow, that didn't fit with my image of the young doctor on his way up. You can get fired for getting the boss's wife upset.

I pulled onto the street behind the LaGrange, and Jana Hefflin from APD communications rang my car phone.

"Jenny, I've been listening in on a call. One of my 911 operators is working. Dr. Randazzo was located about an hour ago. He's dead."

"Damn. What happened?"

"He was shot. Body was in a deep ravine about a half mile from his house. The police aren't calling it homicide yet. They're still investigating."

"You're sure it's Randazzo?"

"Yep. He had identification. Sorry, Jenny."

"Thanks, I appreciate it. I owe you one," I said. I knew Jana had an abiding affection for chocolate-covered strawberries made by a local candy company—Lamme's. I'd make sure she received a box the next time they were offered for sale.

When I got inside, I plopped in a customer chair in front of C.J.'s desk and told her our missing person had been found dead.

She was pulling apart sheets of computer paper as they came out of the printer. "Should we call Marta Randazzo?"

"We'll wait. The police have to make their notifications."

We discussed my conversations with Tiffany, and when the printer's clatter abruptly stopped, C.J. held up the pages. "I came up with more info about Mrs. Randazzo. She comes from an old West Texas ranching family. She inherited more money than you or I could ever imagine.

"I think," she added, "Dr. Lansen changed horses in midstream. When he realized Randazzo was losing the lawsuit and the medical practice would go down the tubes, he figured Marta was his best bet. She's got enough money to set up two or three practices. And personally, I think young Lansen is involved right up to his pretty blue eyes," said C.J.

I thought about how Marta and Chris Lansen had acted when we were there. C.J. could be right. *If* Chris wanted to get ahead and if he felt Marta could help. But I didn't think Marta was involved. She had seemed genuinely worried about Tony's disappearance and, besides, I liked her. "No, I can't buy it."

"Why not?" C.J. prided herself on her judgment of people, and she got a little huffy because I didn't agree. "Look, he's hot after the missus and he probably saw a quick and dirty way to take out the husband." She was working up her theory, hoping to convince me. "He probably began stalking Marta to use as a cover for his real target . . ."

When I said I couldn't buy it, I meant I couldn't buy Marta's involvement. I did have many doubts about Chris Lansen. "Possibly. He says he went out looking for Randazzo. Maybe he found him and killed him."

"The stalking tale could have been just that, a tale."

"What about your 'Good Buddy,' Bernard?" I asked. "His wife's infidelity could have sent him into a jealous rage. Or what about the woman scorned, Sonja Bernard?"

C.J. said, "Bernard might strike out in the heat of passion if he caught his wife with Tony. But he's a drunk, and I doubt he'd have the balls to plan anything sophisticated.

"And Mrs. Bernard is cut from the same mold as Randazzo. She's played around for years, but she always goes back to her husband. He needs her."

"Surely you didn't find that out from your computer," I said.

"No, I called Carolyn Martin. She filled me in on the Bernards."

My friend, Carolyn, who's hip-deep in society happenings, knew all about the skeletons in the jet-setters' closets. If Carolyn said Sonja had the morals of a rock-star groupie, then it was true. "Okay, so where does that leave us?"

C.J. stared at me. "Back to Marta Randazzo. She's one cool bitch."

"No, I think she's putting on a front. Acting cool when she really isn't." The more I thought about it, the more I felt I was right. "Marta couldn't kill—"

"Listen to you, Jenny, listen to that nonsense coming from your mouth. The husband abused her regularly, he played around—even had an affair with a friend." C.J.'s tone was curt. "Chris Lansen and Marta Randazzo together," she said. "They have the best motive, and Chris sure had the opportunity."

I thought about the vulnerability I had seen in Marta's eyes and was determined to give her every benefit of the doubt. "If Chris did it, he was acting alone."

"No way. Marta is involved, believe me. She was fed up with her husband." C.J. shook her finger at me and raised her voice. "Randazzo acted like a horse's ass routinely. Now he's lost his medical practice. Suddenly, Marta and Chris both see a solution to all their problems."

"Dammit, we don't even know yet that it was murder. Maybe Randazzo killed himself. What do the police say?"

C.J. shrugged.

"Take it from me—if Randazzo was murdered, Marta didn't do it." I stood and walked out of the reception area and into my inner office, slamming the door behind me.

Once inside I started cooling off immediately. I've always been that way. I can get angry enough to chew nails, spout off, then quickly my anger subsides. When C.J. began to get angry with me, I should've backed off. It was stupid, and I knew it.

My partner can stay mad for hours—days even. The only way to head it off was to try and make her laugh. If I could get her to laugh, things would smooth out quickly.

I stayed in my office for about five minutes, rehearsing what I would say to C.J., but when I went back out to her desk in reception—she was gone.

She'd left a note saying she'd gone to APD to see what she could find out from Larry Hays. Hoo-boy, I thought. When she's too angry to tell me when she's leaving, she's really mad.

Lieutenant Hays worked in homicide, and he'd been my late husband's partner and best friend. After Tommy died Larry took on the role of my brother/protector. For a private investigator, having a friend on the force was a huge bonus. If Larry hadn't worked on the Randazzo case, he'd know who had and would be able to give C.J. all the inside dope.

Talking to Larry was another good way for C.J. to get over her anger. If she could talk shop with him, she'd chill out fast.

I tidied up my desk, set the answering machine and left.

But instead of going home, I found myself heading to the Randazzos'. Something about Marta pushed my buttons, and I had to see if I could find out why.

Marta Randazzo wasn't particularly glad to see me, but she didn't slam the door in my face. She just said, "Come in, if you like." I followed her down the hall to the den.

Once again I had the feeling I'd been in this room before; the Indian colors and Kachina Dolls and arrowheads were so familiar it was spooky. I refused the drink she offered and sat down.

Marta certainly didn't look like a woman who only a few hours ago had learned of her husband's death. Her make-up was impeccable. No red eyes or tears. Her whole demeanor was changed; she acted poised and self-assured. She picked up her glass and drank, standing regally by the fireplace, and then stared at me over the rim. "You expected tears?" Her tone was defiant.

"Everyone handles grief differently."

"I can't pretend grief when there's nothing there. I can't pretend when deep down I'm glad Tony's dead."

Suddenly, I was ten years old again, and memories came flooding back. My mother and I were at my aunt's house, in her living room decorated with Indian artifacts. Decorated much like this room was.

I could even hear my mother's voice. It sounded tearful and sad. "Everyone handles grief differently."

I recalled Aunt Patsy saying, "I can't pretend grief when deep down I'm glad Stoney is dead."

My mother said, "But Patsy, I don't understand. What did you do?"

Both of my aunt's eyes were blackened, and she had a plaster cast on her arm. I'd never seen anyone look so defiant. Aunt Patsy said, "I killed him. I got his pistol and I shot him. I just couldn't take the beatings anymore. Not with this baby coming."

"Shhh," said my mother, turning to me. "Jenny, why don't you go play outside. Aunt Patsy and I need to talk grown-up stuff."

I sat there, stunned, as it all rushed back. I could now remember everything I'd blocked out. My aunt being arrested, and there was a trial or something. Later, she was sent away, probably to a women's prison. She didn't even come to my mother's funeral three years later. Maybe she couldn't if she was in prison, but as a child I didn't know that. I only knew how hurt I was because she wasn't there. I'd been crazy about Aunt Patsy. I guess I couldn't deal with all the emotional trauma and had buried it. Until I met Marta Randazzo.

I looked at Marta. "You killed him, didn't you? You killed him because he beat you and cheated on you and you'd finally had enough. His affair with Sonja Bernard was the last straw."

Marta began shaking her head no, but I continued. "You wanted a way out."

"No," she said. And for the first time since I'd met her, she stood straight with her shoulders back. "He scarred Ellen Davis's face, but he wasn't sorry. He even laughed about it. Just like he laughed over what he did to me." Marta pulled her sweater up and off her head in one fluid motion. She was braless, and I winced at the misshapen breasts and the hideous red surgical scar tissue.

"See! See what he did to me?" She was crying now and could barely speak. "I-I killed him . . . be-because I didn't want him to get away with ruining another woman."

"But he didn't . . ."

"Y-you think giving Ellen Davis thousands of dollars could ever be enough? And it didn't even faze him. He was going to disappear. Move to another state and start all over. Start butchering women again. I couldn't let him. I-I had to stop him."

"So, that's why you had a blind spot about her. What

did you do when she just up and confessed?" asked C.J.

"I told Marta I knew one of the best defense lawyers in Texas. I called Bulldog Porter. He came over and together they drove downtown to police headquarters." I looked at C.J. "Thanks for not reminding me how right you were."

She shrugged. "What about Marta being stalked?"

"Randazzo probably set that up for his disappearing act."

"And Chris Lansen wasn't involved?"

"Bulldog wouldn't let Marta talk to me. I believe Chris dumped the body for her, but killing Tony was her own solitary act."

I thought about that Dinah Washington song then. "Marta sure had a front row seat for her revenge."